WHAT GOES R♀UND...

WHAT GOES R♀UND...

'Feminine power is perpetual, cyclic but beyond recon for most women. That oblivion confines them to an eternal illusion of their servile bondage to the entire humanity...'

Dr. Sashikala

PARTRIDGE
A Penguin Random House Company

Copyright © 2015 by Dr. Sashikala.

ISBN:	Hardcover	978-1-4828-5700-9
	Softcover	978-1-4828-5699-6
	eBook	978-1-4828-5698-9

Print information available on the last page.

To order additional copies of this book, contact
Partridge India
000 800 10062 62
orders.india@partridgepublishing.com

www.partridgepublishing.com/india

DEDICATED TO

Every man who respects his woman.

This work of fiction is based on what many women I know have been experiencing. All the characters that appear in the book, excepting one, are drawn from real life. Hence, their semblance to any person dead or alive is not intentional but incidental.

Contents

About the Author- *Dr.Sashikala*

Dr. Sashikala has been an academician for 27 years. She could successfully ride more than two horses- taking care of her personal life, periodic academic enhancement, literary pursuit and career-simultaneously. With two Ph.Ds, one in English and the other in Education, she ensured that her teaching career ended when she resigned from the post of the Principal of a reputed college in Coimbatore, the day she qualified for her second Ph.D. degree.

All along, she has been writing quite a bit, but never thought of becoming a published writer. Her rambling had invoked quite a lot of appreciation and her close circle of friends had, time and again implied that she would be a hit with her fluid and straight style of writing, but she had not given it a thought so long.

Sashi is now an expert-trainer and imparts communication and behavioural training to different people. Her ability to move her trainees through stories during the motivational talks, sowed the seeds for her desire to get published. Of course, she too had a story close to her heart, which she had always wanted to tell the world.

Acknowledgements

Getting to see one's work in print calls for a tremendous effort that goes way beyond the writer's alone. It is a kind of revelation. I understand that just a writer and her story alone would not suffice for publication.

I owe a lot to my family that did not explicitly record any surprise or shock when I declared that I was going to write a book and get it published. In fact, every one of them reacted as if it was a very normal thing expected of me. I owe for that to all of you - my son Niranjan Aathreya and his wife Janani, my brother Ravi Shankar, sister Lakshmi Gopal and my mom Vijaya Radhakrishnan.

Well, I do miss my dad who would have been my worst critic and ensured a much better quality in my treatment of the subject matter! His role was assumed by his grandson and it was Niranjan Aathreya who made me go back, every time I decided that the work was done. His blatant criticisms and sensible suggestions on the plot, diction and characterisation and most important of all, his creative ideas in designing the cover, have ensured a niche for me as a writer. Niranjan, you are part of the book in every sense!

A big thanks to my daughter-in-law Janani Aathreya for just being there and cheering me up.

Manasvi Aathreya is my source of inspiration and strength and, thanks baby for making your timely appearance.

I owe a great deal to all the real people around from whose inspiration I have drawn all the characters in my book-both the good and the not so good men and women- excepting one!

I have made frequent mention of composers and performing artists like Igor Stravinsky, Anton Dvorak, George Bizet, Ilayaraja, ABBA, Dr. Balamuralikrishna, Brian Adams and Pankaj Udhas in various parts of the book to indicate the period, calibre as well as the age of the characters.

I am very thankful to Partridge Publications, who could translate my impulsive decision to publish my work, into a reality, by rendering all required support.

Foreword

What Goes Round... is essentially a woman centric work of fiction based on instances drawn from real-time experience. I am the story teller, but it can be anybody's story. The characters are drawn from the typical Indian scenario, in which conformity takes precedence over personal likes and dislikes in the life of most Indian women. Every one of the so-called happily married women would have paid a very heavy price for the comfort-zone that cocoons her, without realising what she has lost. When a woman resists the imposed changes and tries to retain at least a bit of her real self, life takes her on a roller-coaster ride and hardly a few disembark without losing their orientation. This is the story of such triumphant survivors.

Originally, the twelve episodes making up the four parts were meant to be short stories. They are penned in such a way that each gives a sense of completion, when read separately, without the mention or influence of any other previous or succeeding episodes. The novel reiterates the cyclic nature of life and hence the end of one of these characters marks the beginning of another. Further, the four episodes pertaining to either Gina or Ranjani or Shree will make up complete reading materials, individually. This book can, therefore, be read as twelve short stories or three long stories or as a single novel.

The three names given to womanhood- Gina, Ranjani and Shree- present the different facets of our women in general, irrespective of the social status and cultural orientation. In fact, I have personally gone through the lives of these three protagonists and for that matter, most of our women will identify with any or all the characters at some point of time.

This novel is my earnest attempt to show that 'life' has no gender, and it is the passion to experience everything that one encounters during the journey, that makes life meaningful and worth living. This is not just an exaltation of womanhood, but also a sincere tribute to all men who have the right perspective of a woman!

-SASHIKALA RADHAKRISHNAN.

OVERTURE

What Goes Round...

H_e was a being of extraordinary perceptions and exceptional sensitivity. The quest in him to know the forbidden and possess the mysterious had driven him restless and relentless in his pursuit. He was there in the much dreaded place just for one last time, in an attempt to accomplish the unthinkable.

The scene around, complete with the sight of the flocking visitors and the cacophony of the other earthly creatures did not belong in his world. He was focused on his unattainable mission, no matter how impossible and ridiculous it would seem.

There was copious lore of her charm and magnificence, her ability to enchant and possess. He had heard them all and decided that she would be his, ultimately, as he was aware of his own unique prowess. So, he decided to linger in wait in this haunt in what appeared to be the longest ever epoch.

He kept his mission his treasured secret, lest he should be admonished and dissuaded. His elders and peers often wondered the long durations of his disappearance and he always managed to assuage their curiosity with an intelligent quip, letting them believe that his aesthetic pursuit had driven him to isolation from the community.

He waited and waited for what passed off as ages, but in his existence, time had been standing still, hanging in a tranquil *era that looked like an eternity, just waiting for that one moment.*

He was forlorn, torn between hope and dejection- he was hopeful of her coming there but dejected by the fact that it would be the remotest possibility, as always.

She must have sensed him- his intentions- and must have decided to taunt him and finally haunt him. Or, had she decided to drive him away through deprivation and disappointment?

He was thinking these weird thoughts for the thousandth time, may be, because he was driven right to the brink of disillusion and just then he saw her!

He was totally unprepared for the sudden vista that offered a fascinating feast to his perplexed awareness, and still, he could not believe his eyes! Were his eyes playing tricks on him? His rambling mind went blank and his thoughts and vision focused on the incredible spectre emerging in front.

She came gliding into the glade all too suddenly!

She was not like anything he had anticipated, thought of or heard of, but still, she was bewitching. The dark eyes and long strands of hair highlighted her fair countenance. He was surprised by her strange attire, and more so, her stranger attitude and he asked himself, 'Is she the one?'

No matter what, no matter who, he knew that his wait was over and that it was really worth a wait. He concluded that she was the one even if she were really not to be.

He wanted to plunge into action and get hold of her but had to desist the impulse as her forthcoming actions jolted him out of his wits. She looked cool and composed but her darting eyes and restless saunter betrayed her disposition.

Obviously, she was waiting too!

Yes! He could read all those telltale symptoms, having gone through that tormenting anguish all along.

She too seemed to have come with a quest and now settled to linger in wait. Her frequent fleeting glances towards the tree gave her an air of edginess.

He was hesitant and decided to wait and watch. She was totally oblivious of his presence, sat down by the rounded tree and got engrossed in the surrounding.

He peered and peered and caught sidelong glances of her.

He gazed and gazed and got lost!

He stared and stared and got enchanted!

He gaped and gaped and got entrapped!

He peeked from his hiding place and got transfixed to the spot for an eternity!

She too was lost deep into her realm and he tried to follow her.

He was still reeling under the impact of the initial shock he had experienced, the first moment he set his eyes on her. It was just impossible to find such a creature in those parts. She had an air of absolute autonomy, with a total lack of trepidation of any sort.

Her world must have been exclusive and exquisite and he realised that to enter it would tantamount to trespass and to possess her would pose the biggest challenge, as it would amount to first breaking her spirit of gay abandon.

'Who is she and what is she?' He slowly ambled towards the thorny bushes on the left to get a still better and closer view. Just as he hid himself fully, she looked up and threw a cursory glance in his direction, jumped up and seconds later, he could catch the sight of her gliding away- slowly this time.

He waited... expecting her to turn around and take a look at him, for he was now standing in the open. Her presence simply vanished, but he felt her close by, all over the place.

She was all around him and inside him, choking him and benumbing his senses. The pervasive intrusion into his benumbed senses came as a real shocker and he was reeling under its impact. He was caught totally unawares and he struggled to wriggle out of the overpowering dominion, but failed miserably!

Suddenly, he stopped struggling and ended the ongoing ordeal. He yielded himself completely to her consuming intensity and succumbed in a sweet surrender.

Hardly had he realized then that he was taken.

He, who wanted to possess, had been possessed.

PART I

THAT'S ME!

1

It's not that easy!

The wait was getting intolerable though the surroundings proved to be surrealistic, rather too good to be true. In fact, the extraordinary elements around the terrible tamarind tree failed to elicit the kind of reaction that should have emanated from Gina. Her focus was the tree and her roving eyes swept through the green foliage. She was clutching her Algebra notebook tightly in the left hand and held a pen between her fingers and her entire body was in a state of high alert, ready to scoot. Her bicycle *Tiga*, also in a state of readiness, was just leaning on a cylindrical stone left half buried in the red earth adjacent to the tree, in case she decided to jump on it and scurry.

Gina checked her watch again, the old one that had belonged to her *Ammamma* for more than thirty years.

It was passed down to her when *Ammamma* got a new HMT from her daughter, Gina's mother. That had been one more thing that really had infuriated Gina. *Amma* once again had proved that Gina was the least of her concerns, for it was Gina who had wanted a watch all along and when she accompanied *Amma* and helped in the selection, well she was pretty sure that it was for her, but was heart-broken and inconsolable on learning that it had to go to *Ammamma*. Why should an old lady be given so much of importance in our households? What if she was turning sixty, even the Jack tree in the garden was almost eighty- or that's what people said!

Restlessness was writ all over her form and absent-mindedly she shifted her gaze from the tree and looked ahead and what she saw actually got registered in her mind this time and nearly knocked her senses hard. It had been right there in front of her and how did she miss all these? Had she gone deaf and blind simultaneously? She became aware of the cacophony of mixed cackles all on a sudden. What a sight! This was the least of her expectations and, what kind of a one-track mind she had!

Her initial fear for the tamarind tree and her mission had both vapourised from her mind all on a sudden and her senses got engrossed in her environment.

Gina now found herself absorbed in what she saw in the pond in front. The pond had turned to a muddy puddle with all kinds of shrubs sprouting out. May be, it could not be called a pond as there had never been any lotus or lily creeper, like you would often find in the regular ones in her place. Even in terms of dimensions, it was much bigger, shapeless and had no definite boundaries. Well it was not big enough to be called a lake too. Without wasting a second thought over the nomenclature issue she looked on.

Gina was stunned by the commotion and confusion that was prevailing right in the vicinity. What were these and where had they come from? She forgot all about the purpose of her visit to that eerie place and her preposterous mission obviously got abandoned now. Her excitement got the better of her and found her shaking and looking bewildered. She made a cry which was neither a 'pooh' nor a 'wow' and stifled it half way through. She had no business to be there, but there she was!

It just was fantastic and slowly and unobtrusively, she started edging sideways to the shade of the lone tamarind tree and slipped to a sitting posture, leaning against the rough trunk. God! How do people manage to sit under such trees and whisper words of love and tenderness, like in the movie she had seen the previous day with *Paattima* (this, her father's mom who lived in their house permanently, unlike *Ammamma* who visited once in two years for a three-month's stay)? Won't the stupid lovers ever get bitten by those mean, angry black-ants or irritated or distracted by other creepy bugs and insects that kept crawling all over you?

Now, all those tiny creatures had suddenly and totally gone out of Gina'a mind and she was so absorbed by the pond (lake?). She was able to see long bills and legs of different hues and shapes. Obviously migratory birds! What were they doing there? Must be nesting! She could make out a few of them, crane, heron, stork, well *appa* had once shown the pictures when they had been to Connemara Library during their visit to her aunt's place in Madras (Chennai now). But that was just once. Look at her predicament. There was so much to experience but hardly enough words to define everything.

Gina opened her notebook. There were about twenty blank pages and she started writing down the description of every species of bird she could spot. She must be thorough this time. When you tried to tell *Appa* something, he invariably asked too many questions. Why should he give so much of importance to details and in the end call her a frivolous fool? Well this time it would not be so, for she would present him with all details.

The quacking and cackling sounds were ranting the air and the November sky turned darker with more clouds.

Gina was fully engrossed in her mission. Other than the cacophony of the winged visitors there was no other sound excepting the occasional whrooming of a truck or a bus, once in a way, on the big road about a miles away, which actually was a highway.

Suddenly a chill ran through her rather rounded body – well she was not fat but at the same time could not be termed slender too- and she became aware of her surroundings. Involuntarily she jumped up and moved away from the tree. She thought she saw some form moving towards the tree, or were her senses playing tricks on her perceptions?

She suddenly turned around and surveyed the surroundings, especially the tree. She caught glimpse of a bunch of leaves fluttering in a bush to the left of the tree about fifteen yards away.

She was surprised at not finding any vegetation right under or around the tree.

Again she threw a cursory glance at the bush.

Nothing or no one!

But she kept getting the eerie feeling that she was not alone there.

What had she been doing there?

'O my God!' Gina shook herself up and with a startled expression checked her watch. It was four thirty five. She had been sitting in that God forsaken place for nearly five hours.

'It's well past coffee time'. She remembered the onion *bajjis Amma* had been talking about during brunch- they normally had full meals on holidays like this particular day, by around eleven.

People must be wondering where she had gone. Would they miss her? May be they would think that she must have curled up with some book in her favourite spot in the 'Book Room', where *Appa* had stacked rows and rows of books in huge shelves. That was her cubby-hole in the house and she enjoyed crawling into the books and losing herself amidst the pages when she was not out on one of her expeditions riding *Tiga*.

Gina simply straightened her cotton pants and the loose shirt she was wearing. Taking long strides, she reached her bicycle and threw her note-book and pen into the basket hitched to *Tiga's* handle-bar. With one push she got the bike straight, sat astride and started peddling hard. A steep climb up brought her out of that gloomy wooded area and manoeuvring through the almost non-existent, narrow, tar road she reached home- but not quite!

What was that crowd in front of the huge gate? Something tightened in the pit of her stomach, what's wrong really? She peddled faster, strands of her long hair coming out of the confining rubber-band were flailing all over her face. Some brat, looked like Muthu, the fisherman's son, shrieked, *'Akka'* (Sister)!

All eyes turned in her direction and there was a hushed silence. Anxious looking *Amma* emerged from the crowd and just looked at her. Gina froze a bit at the vivid anger glowering on her face and the scorn in her eyes that almost bordered contempt. Cringing inward Gina wished that she had turned invisible.

'Where had you been Gina?'-this was *Paattima*; Gina heaved a sigh of relief. Nothing wrong with the old lady as she had originally feared, and obviously the crowd was there for a different reason and not on account of her. Even though the granddaughter's and grandmother's ways with each other always exuded an air of bellicosity, both shared moments of warmth, especially when they set out to watch a movie in *Lakshmi Theatre* twice a week. The theater screened two-year old movies and each one would be screened for just three or four days. May be this was one such moment. The old woman did a strange thing. She lunged forward, clung to Gina and started weeping. The short lady's top-knot came up to Gina's nostrils, tickling her and she had to control her giggles.

'What the hell is wrong with these people?'

'Look at her, see the way she dresses and riding a cycle all the time- more like a boy'- this was the next- door *Aachi* who would never let go a chance to take a dig at Gina and her siblings. She never approved of Gina's jeans, stretch pants or handloom shirts.

Gina gave her a sweet smile, disentangled herself from the old lady's hold and simply asked, 'When are you making *paal kozhukkattai* next, *Aachi?* Don't forget to send some as usual'.

The lady was taken aback, 'Where did you go, girl?'

'Kothankadu', the moment the word came out of her mouth, there was a heavy silence followed by hushed 'oooh's and 'aaah's.

'Gina, is there no limit to your fool-hardiness? You know that place is haunted. Every afternoon the *Muni* comes to the tamarind tree to rest. Why are you not normal? He could have slapped you or possessed you. You wouldn't then be talking like this', this was Meena *Akka* who lived in the next street, right behind their house. In fact she liked Gina very much and still treated her like a kid sister.

'Ahaaaa... I forgot...', Gina ran inside, abandoning *Tiga* propped against the wall. Till then, it had not occurred to her that she, or rather her mysterious disappearance, had been the concern of all those gathered there.

'Appaaaa...', she knew where to find him. He was in his den with his Veena across his lap, stretching out his right leg in front of him and folding the other. He sat leaning on the wall and with his eyes closed, playing the out-line of some *raaga*.

'Chaarukesi!', Gina shouted out her guess as she stepped into the den. *'Appaaaaa…'*

Appa's eyes flung open and with an irritated smile he looked at her. Probably the din and throng outside the gate had not reached him or he had been oblivious of them. That was what was great about that house! Inside of the nine-foot tall wooden gate, it was a totally different world, her comfort zone. All members of the household would talk and behave different and related to each other on a different plane once the gates closed behind them. There was solidarity in all conversations and dealings, with *Appa* assuming captainship, being a natural.

'I have told you not to run inside the house like this. See the ground is shaking under your feet', he chided her as usual.

But Gina was not her usual sensitive self and did not give the well expected reaction of pulling a long

17

face and stomping away. She did not seem to hear his sarcastic hints implying that she was plump.

'*Appa*, you won't believe what I saw. There were hundreds of them...thousands. And the noise they were making...'

'Wait, wait, won't you ever start anything from the beginning, silly girl? Who was making noise? And where?'

'Birds, in *Kothan*kadu!'

Appa looked perplexed. 'What? When did you go there and why?' he demanded.

She started getting a creepy feeling when she suddenly sensed the hint of anger in his voice.

What a fool she had been! *Kothan*kadu was out of bounds for anybody, especially girls, in the afternoons. This tenet was upheld as a sacred, unwritten rule in her place, which was neither a town nor a village. Although a rationalist, her father never questioned local sentiments and ensured that no one in the household violated those local codes. A great conformist apparently and this sometimes made Gina uneasy.

Gina swallowed hard, took a step back and blurted. 'No *Appa*, all were talking about that *Puliamara Muni*. I wanted to just catch a glimpse of him and if possible get an interview and I even went prepared with a note-book to jot down whatever he would say and of course, I remembered to take a pen too'.

At least, *Appa* would not think that she was half-baked and would appreciate her preparedness and forethought.

But what she saw on his face rather dismayed her. He had a look of disbelief and obviously he was flabbergasted.

'What, interview the *Muni?* My foot!'

Without wasting a moment she cut in when he paused a bit and spoke very fast. '*Appa*, yesterday you told us all to think about our future and start preparing from now on. I thought and thought and this morning I decided that I'd do well as an investigative journalist and as a first step decided to have some practice and so…' she abruptly stopped on seeing his bemused look change into something more serious.

'*Appa, Muni* didn't come today, probably he stays away on holidays, but I saw those birds, cranes, geese, storks, herons, pelicans and a lot more. See I have carefully noted down every detail about every species in the notebook I had taken with me.' She opened the page and thrust it in front.

Appa's expression changed totally all on a sudden. He pushed aside the notebook and like a child he clapped his hands twice.

'Migratory birds? Come let's go there.'

Gina did not understand how one could suddenly get into a shirt that was flung on the arm of the chair so fast and simultaneously don a different mood faster.

'Come Gina,' he dragged her by her hand so fast that she almost lost balance and stumbled. He did not care. His hands let go of her and without even bothering to check if she was following right behind, he rushed out, saw *Tiga*, got on the seat and shouted 'Get on the back', and started peddling. By then the crowd outside the gate had dispersed, probably after giving her mother a sermon on how to bring girls up, inside locked premises.

Gina had barely jumped on the carrier, sat astride and adjusted herself giving the bicycle a violent shake, when her father started moving his legs faster. The dusk had been rendered gloomier by the trees around and as the bicycle glided down the ramp into the wood the noise grew louder and clearer.

'They are more in number now', Gina yelled in excitement.

'Silly girl, instead of wasting your time writing descriptions of the birds, you ought to have come straight home and we could have seen them well in broad daylight. Yes, you are right, oh... saw it? That's an egret. Do you see the fellow on the bush at the extreme right?'

'The grey one, pa?'

'No. That white thing on the extreme right. It is called Asian Open bill.'

It was becoming difficult to see. So, the rule applied for not just cats, but birds too! They all looked grey in the dark! The tamarind tree silhouetted in the growing dark had turned quite eerie. She held her breath and a shiver ran through her form; her hands automatically folded tight in front of her.

Appa grew silent and looked intently at her. A look of understanding dawned on his face. 'So, that's it, all these stories about *Munis* and *Mohinis,* to keep people away from this place so that these birds would be left in peace.' He nodded his head slowly.'

'Who is *Mohini, pa?*'

'She is supposed to scare away the boys just as the *Muni* scares the girls away.'

So, *he* is not real! Gina was disappointed. 'I thought *he* was there all along.'

Her father looked at her affectionately and casually, with his voice overwhelming with mischief, said, 'Can't be sure! One day or other *he* might even spring you a surprise and present *himself* and offer his services to you.'

Then he simply changed the topic, 'So you want to be an investigative journalist? Ha ha ha… Who ever told you that interviewing the *Muni* would make you one? Silly girl, high time you grew up. You are fifteen, remember?'

'Sixteen, this July', she mumbled.

2

I wallow in myself!

$Y_{uck!}$

Ranjani looked at the disgusting creature snoring at the other end of the big double cot and burst into tears for the nth time. Luckily it was not an everyday-oops... every night- affair and heart of hearts she was grateful to her guardian angel who had wielded a huge protective shield around her with just a small gap for the creepy creature to slink into the premises of her pristine privacy, just once in a way.

Again she rushed into the bathroom wanting to throw up. Well there was nothing left any more. She felt hollowed inside the veneer of her dirty deceptive self, which, she knew, would shatter to pieces at a simple tap. She looked at her face in the mirror and was shocked to see the hue of darkness encircling the round eyes rendering it darker.

Tears welled in those large eyes, tears of self-pity, droplets of inadequacy, floods of poor self worth- she picked up the cake of soap and threw it at her image, 'Dirty bitch!' Plomp! It slithered all over the floor on which it fell off like a dead rat finally. Nothing around her seemed to be alive. The nauseating stench of death was pouring in from all corners of that quite house stifling her so much, that her breath started getting shallower.

'Calm down, you stupid woman, don't overdo it! One of these days you would go overboard', she told the person staring at her from the looking glass and was surprised to see those words echoed back. She stripped and stood under the icy waters of the shower.

'Calm down, you've got a long way to go, strong girl', she gasped not being able to bear the intensity of the chill spray that spewed needles on her. She just pictured herself, pierced by millions of icy needles all over, bleeding but with no sleuth for the blood to flow out. She appeared scary in her vision, with silvery spikes jutting out and rolled all over her form like a mat.

'Let that skunk try to get closer now', she smirked at the imagination of the great pain she would then be able to inflict on that animal.

Wrapped in her towel, she tip-toed into the room and softly opened her cupboard and pulled out a nightie from the top shelf.

Her hair was dripping wet and quietly opening the door of her bedroom, she stepped out, but stopped short seeing the old man standing near the main door.

The luminous hands of the clock on the wall opposite said that it was two twenty.

Okay! This must be the second or third round of his routine checking of the main door. His OCD was getting the better of him, and he made it a point to check the locks once in two hours at least. Ranjani moved sideways and stealthily clambered towards the staircase. Reaching the landing on the top, she felt with her left foot for Nila's bed. Nila, was stretched on her sides with her tail tucked between the hind legs and just raised her head seeing Ranjani approach. Nila was by then quite accustomed to this nocturnal routine of her patron. The terrace door would be opened silently, and she would go out and start pacing up and down, Nila would follow her once and then choose an unobtrusive spot to settle down. After getting tired of walking she would slump on the floor, mostly close to her foster child and patting her head, would either burst into tears or start talking in a low sonorous voice.

Nila understood, not what she said, but definitely the pathos and her mood, and tried to comfort her by licking her hands and face.

'Good girl. Nila! Just listen to me. Never ever get married. You will be doomed for life. O my God! What am I doing? Advising a bitch right in the middle of the night- what is happening to me?'

Her initial feeling of disgust was almost gone but she was still seething with raw anger, more at her inability to do anything about anything. She could successfully frustrate the insensitive beast that called itself her husband, by her sheer indifference. What had initially looked like submission to him was actually her retaliation. She had gone to a sordid state of self-abnegation, a state past caring what happened to her, especially when he tried to prove his manhood and prowess by mere physical dominance. All the while, her cold, frigid response would dampen his fortitude and they would know that it was an irrevocable stale mate.

She got up so suddenly, that Nila, who was edging towards her slowly, intending to put her head on the soft lap, was disappointed and abruptly got up and ran towards her cozy bed.

Ranjani came down after carefully latching up the door. Her hair had dried in the breeze and was now in a messy tangle. She eyed the clock sideways on reaching the bottommost step and realised that she had spent seventy minutes up in the open terrace. She then looked in the direction of the diffused light that suddenly appeared to her left.

'Nandhu, you gave me a fright! What are you doing at the fridge at three thirty in the morning?'

'And you Ranji, what business did you have in the terrace at this time?' He had nowadays stopped calling her 'mom'. 'By the way, don't call me Nandhu as if I'm a wee little kid.'

The equations between them had changed all on a sudden and they found themselves at an equal footing of comradeship.

'Aa haa… I was having a rendezvous with my paramour who came up the rope-ladder.'

'Thought as much! So I'll hope for a step-dad. Let your choice be good at least this time… or else, I will kill you'.

Conversations of this kind were becoming more and more frequent now a days, between mother and son. The boy was too sharp not to notice her swollen eyes even in the dim light pouring out of the fridge. Each could sense the pain the other was going through but chose not to address any issue. That was what had bound them and brought them closer. Further, they knew the futility of addressing issues, thereby killing those lighter moments, which revived their hopes and happiness. They were suffering the same evil but each in his or her own terms!

She looked at his form and could not help thinking, 'what a fine lad he is turning out to be, inheriting the strong physique of his father!' She held her breath and whispered a stealthy wish. 'Let the semblance stop with just the appearance'.

'What did you say?' he asked stuffing the big chunk of cake he had just raided, into his mouth.

Before she could say anything, the door opposite opened and the old lady emerged adjusting her specs. 'Mother and son! Won't you give the household some peace even past mid-night? What do you chatter about the whole time? It is not manners to talk what normal people don't understand, when you live in the middle of others. What is it now?'

Ranjani paled. This old woman could get rather nasty with her tongue.

Obviously she was the worst hit by her husband's OCD, which had bestowed moments of embarrassment, especially, when suddenly some one of her own relatives made it a regular practice to cite anyone of those hilarious incidents during family functions to break the monotony pervading the imposing atmosphere.

Usually, one of Raju's cousins would remind the others of an archaic incident when, the old man (much younger at that time) had occupied one of the two available bathrooms during some family function and had stayed inside even until after the remaining twenty or so people had all got ready using the other one, and how, finding him still inside, they all had locked him up in the house and left for the function hall. Everyone would break into peels of giggles and laughter and add bits and pieces of information to complete the story as to how, when they all returned after three hours, they had found him slowly putting on the last button of his shirt and asking them if everybody else was ready to go for the function.

Initially, Ranjani had been shocked at the insensitivity of that crowd around, not because they were targeting her father-in-law, but because she found their attitude so gross and disgusting. They all lacked the decency to abstain from launching personal attacks on others simply because self-expression and the great love to be heard were the inherent trait of every one of them, including the kids. Later she realized that, inspite of their social status and their comfortable standards of life-style, they still were a crude lot, with their roots still running strong and deep near some jungles and they had a total lack of sophistication. Even she was not spared. Very often her preference for simplicity in matters of attire and jewellery drew sarcastic comments from women her age, but she never bothered to retaliate or waste her time and efforts in defending herself, and also she knew very well that nothing better could be expected of the entire lot. Her father once called them *rich but gaudy.* But Ranjani refuted him with the comment, 'No *pa.* These dumbos travel Business Class in *Air Emirates,* all the while not forgetting to carry their curd-rice *dubbas* for dinner. They might be stinking rich but lack class. Yet, they can't be called bad- may be a bit crude, a little weird and grossly unrefined in certain ways.'

On the personal front, the old woman had been the worst hit, which Ranjani had suspected the moment she observed that the old couple slept on separate beds in the same room.

All on a sudden, after the first eight years of marriage and after begetting three children, the old man's OCD had started showing so badly, that he was very careful to avoid any sort of contact with his wife, whom he thought was the generator of all dirt and filth in the house. He would spend long hours in the bathroom, washing his hands and wiping his feet. That had made the lady rather bitchy and it was then that she had started turning all her rancour and acrimony on all apparently happily married women around her, excepting her own daughters, and had finally ensured that Ranjani would never ever experience the blessings of conjugal bliss in that house right from the start. She could successfully infuse her own bitterness into her doting son, who had now formulated the equation that being a good husband would tantamount to being a disloyal son.

Taking pity on the pathetic plight of the old man Ranjani tried to suggest an appointment with a psychiatrist for him, but was immediately silenced by the entire family and the best part was the old man joined the others in the squabbling that followed and his voice was the loudest of all!

Now, the grandson did not care a bit about his venom-spewing grandmother. On the contrary, he in his cheery tone quipped, '*Paatti* its almost four, time to sing a lullaby for your husband. He must have finished his third round, checking the doors. I heard him go into the bathroom one hour back and he should be out in another fifteen minutes. By the time he starts sleeping it will be time to sing *Suprabatham* to your son and get his coffee ready. Don't mind us, we won't interfere with your reign over this house.'

By then Ranjani had slipped into her room and bolted the door from within.

She felt herself stiffen at the mere sight the presence inside. What a stinking bastard! How could her refinement put up with such a gross degenerate son of a bitch? What had that perpetrator of woes done to her, physically and emotionally?

He was an embedded thorn in her tender flesh- one that fed on her and grew inward, stretching into her inner most self, extinguishing her innate passion for life and thus throwing her life to a mere survival mode.

She did not want to think about it now as the day was dawning into yet another Tuesday and she had to work.

She assumed her usual place at the extreme left edge of the bed, turned away from the snoring beast and caught up with whatever was left of her sleep when the familiar words of *Kandhar Sashti Kavasam,* playing in the nearby temple, wafted in through the open window.

> *'Kaakka kaakka Kanaka Vel kaakka'*
> *(May the divine golden Spear protect me)*

3

I am in-charge

'Wanna be young- the rest of my life
Never say no – try anything twice
Till the angels come- and ask me to fly
Gonna be 18 till I die- 18 till I die.'

Bryan Adams was getting too loud and Shree adjusted the volume of the speakers, while singing along and holding the top portion of her jeans with the other hand. The i-pod had a collection which would defy any presumption about the listener. She had music for every mood and had become too dependent on that gadget to give her company. She usually would let it blare when she went into the bathroom for a shower. While getting dressed, it had suddenly occurred to her that the noise was getting on her nerves. As it was, she had been a little jumpy right from the morning for no specific reason, though she knew that she had been waiting for this day.

'Someday I'll be 18, goin' on 55'

As she mouthed the lines she interjected, 'Well, that would be three more years from hence! But look at me, I am more of an anachronism, not behaving my age'.

'Also not looking my age too,' she added slowly as she took a glimpse of her hour-glass image reflected in the looking glass. 5'4" and weighing 63 kilos, full figure, almost flat in the midriff, lovely sparkling eyes, straight nose, voluptuous lower lip, sleek neck, slender legs, muscular arms finely toned with regular work-outs in the gym, one or two graying strands at the temples camouflaged by the trendy burgundy hue, comfy jeans and a clinging top- well, people never believed her age. But, at the same time, she never tried to under-quote it and would always disclose her true age -should someone ask- to her perplexed admirers. That would add up in terms of wisdom and experience and escalated her worth as a self-actualized being- she always would justify.

However, what accentuated her gait and elegance was her stately walk, which gave the impression that she simply glided past any obstacle or rather the obstacle became nonexistent at her approach. She indeed owed her shapely strong legs to the fact that she was so used to walking a lot. Her life had not been a smooth and comfortable one always and she had the habit of walking out of her anger. A disgruntled, seething Shree would set out for a walk and would keep walking, covering mile after mile. The quick short steps, with which she would commence the ritual would slowly transform into long steady strides as the anger and remorse dissipated and drained out of her totally. Sometimes she would find herself in some other part of the big city by the time she got exhausted and would return home in a taxi or take a bus back home, if she had remembered to stuff her wallet into her pocket, with her raging resentment reduced to its residual remains.

Shree searched for the *Citizen* from her collection of watches and beamed when she spotted it.

'Come on, cheer up, you don't need an occasion to receive a gift from your bro,' she remembered the day what her younger brother Pradheep had said so when he suddenly disappeared into the show-room and reemerged with the watch and thrust it into her hands about a couple of years back when they were shopping along with their sister.

Of course, no one could match her sister's fervor for shopping and at times Shree would fling her head in exasperation and say, 'Take it or leave it, but don't ask for my opinion again, as if you would honour it.'

It was on one such occasion, when those two had come down for a short visit, that Pradheep made this gift unexpectedly. It had been more a gesture of solidarity and support, and Shree could read it loud and clear, in spite of the muddled state of affairs that had prevailed around her then.

She stepped into the Pooja room near the dining area. She called it the hope chamber or power room, depending on her mood and occasion, where, according to her, one gets something to cling to even when everything else was apparently lost and the situation had turned bleak. She was not so deep into spirituality as any woman her age normally would tend to be, nor would she demonstrate any ritualistic display of her religious inclination. She had always been fascinated by the brutal, dark, feminine power of *Kali* and, chanting a couple of lines extolling Her, always charged Shree's batteries.

'Kaatyaayinyaaya vitmahe Kanyakumaaryai dimahi Thanno Durgi prachodayaat!

Well, she needed to go in full throttle that day and chanted the *Gayathri* twice more.

Her devotion to *Kali* had elicited varied remarks from the people around. Most of them asked why she could not choose a gentler Deity to protect her. Shree always had felt that one needed to be not only strong but very truthful to feel at ease with this particular Goddess. One could appease any other form of divinity with some kind of rituals and offerings but not this One. She is both the protector and destroyer and the sword and the food-bowl in two of Her many arms indicated this. Of late, Shree had been getting the feeling that it was this faith that had turned her into a dare-devil and she could attribute her own vagrancies to her deep devotion.

'Are you sure? Is that really what you need to do? There should be no U-turn or else I'll throw you out of my house as well as my life', Abi was looking at her intently. They had already gone through this a couple of times before.

'We've wasted enough time, rather, I have', Shree tried to hide the light tremor in her voice. 'Well, this task also can start today.'

'Now what's the program?'

'As planned yesterday, let us finalise the invitation cards to start with, and the other things can follow as per the schedule the three of us had drawn. By the way where is the princess?' Shree always made fun of Mili, for her ways and preferences, as a princess.

'Better we pick her up on the way, or else we would be kept waiting forever', She was quick enough to notice the edginess in his tone and just smiled.

'Then how about your appointment with the advocate?' he added.

'I'll manage. You both take care of the wedding arrangements, let me deal with this essential nuisance myself', Shree tried to smile again but failed.

'Are you kidding? We both had been together through the years and now you want to get rid of me... it's been both our war and I can't send you to the final battle alone'.

'Of course, you are in, but in the initial stages I can manage alone. Give that poor girl a little bit of your precious time, won't you?'

Before he could reply, they heard the rustling of Mili's Anarkali churidar and she stormed in, all smiles.

'Hi, ma!' She came to Shree and struck a pose like one of those models they both were criticizing the previous evening while watching a TV commercial, 'How do you like my new dress? Took me just minutes to select this!'

Abi interjected, 'Ahem... I was the one who selected and paid for this and look at your audacity!'

'Oh, hi *da*, you are here, sorry, I didn't notice.'

'Sorry? Didn't notice? Hmmm… poor me, the prognosis is so obvious…' he started muttering the usual monologue.

Both the ladies joined him in a chorus, 'Both of you will form a league and you are going to forget and forsake me altogether. I have to eat out and probably revert back to my bachelor's days after my marriage'.

Abi tried to glare at them but failed miserably and the three started laughing uncontrollably.

Shree was the first to stop and take a look at the clock. 'Come on, let us get going. It's late already!'

'**Abi** *kutta*, how about this? I like this pink shade and the design is exquisite.' Mili couldn't hide the excitement in her voice, and Shree turned her attention from a card she was holding, and one look at Mili's expression and the card she was clutching, she had an irrepressible impulse to roar into laughter, yet let it out as a nonchalant smile. But, she almost jumped when she heard Abi hollering, holding his stomach and bending forward.

'Grow up baby, whoever told you pink is all girly? That's almost purplish magenta and do you know what that colour stands for?'

Mili's confusion showed and Shree ignored them both and moved away skimming through the variety of cards. She had already decided how she would word the invitation for her chosen group of invitees running to just fifty. This was an acid-test for those who were supposed to be her friends and well wishers. She would know!

'How calculative and opportunistic I have become!' she was shocked and embarrassed a little.

But she could not afford to take any more chances. Just a week ago, she was shattered to bits by the betrayal of trust that she tasted, thanks to the curtsey of her friend of twenty two years, who, fifteen years back, could even furnish a prognosis of the situation she was in, and predict the state of affairs she would find herself in and cautioned her.

Shree winced at the mere thought of Uma, and felt something pricking her eyes. She heaved a huge sigh and tried to focus on the cards, finally chose one at the rear end, probably something most people would not even take a second look at. She could visualize the words, design and alignment and instantly knew it to be the best choice.

She looked around and the boy who had been tagging the trio like a shadow materialised from nowhere.

'M'am has selected', his enthusiasm died on taking a glimpse at the card she held. 'That appears to be so simple and ordinary. People normally don't go in for this stuff.' His disbelief got the better of him and his tone fell flat, rather too flat to sound convincing.

'Yes, that's obvious,' she looked at the poor boy.

'I have a set of words and designs to print, would you like to take a look Madam? I have collected them from numerous websites.'

She just followed him and when he sat in front of the computer, she extended a pen-drive that she had extracted from her jeans pocket and assuaged his bewilderment instantly.

'I have made the required design and composed the words myself. Now let me show you how I need them to appear on the card.'

The poor boy found this too much to pallet. Right from the moment the trio had walked in, he was filled with a strange kind of awe and curiosity and they were full of surprises and hadn't disappointed him in the least.

This hyperactive lady and the young girl passed off as mother and daughter from the way they spoke to each other, but he could not find anything in common- features, complexion, attitude, deportment… no way. Nevertheless, there was something between the young chap and this one; he was sharp enough not to miss the bulk of nonverbal communication that transpired between the guy and the older lady, though he couldn't understand even one bit of it. Even when the girl took out the pink card, he noticed the fleeting smiles exchanged by them just before the lady turned and walked away. Now he could make out the striking semblance, especially the way both smiled. Yes… they must be mother and son… no way! She was too young to be the mother of such a mature looking handsome man. May be sister and brother. Well, the boy and the girl are getting married and…

'Young man! Could you kindly open the folder 'Invitation'? There would be two files and please open the word file named Shree.' He started operating with a jerk and when he obeyed the instructions, he couldn't believe what he saw on the monitor.

Celebrate Life

His eyes roved over the words beneath and he had to make an effort to suppress his 'wow' on learning that the curious duo was indeed mom and son.

The crisp poetic lines were unlike anything he had ever seen on any wedding invitation so far.

'Super M'am! Can you give me the website address? Really, beautiful words!

'So you like them, Arun... that's your name, right? Well, I wrote them. These are special and sincere words I wrote for my friends.'

She went on explaining how she wanted the words on the card, and he couldn't help admiring her more and more. 'Okay, I will need fifty cards.'

'Sorry? Did you say just fifty? Certainly you must be knowing a lot of people and there must be a lot of friends and relatives...' Arun's voice trailed

She gave a hearty laugh, 'Yes I do have a whole heap of them. But who said I want to invite all of them to my son's wedding reception?'

He was at a loss, 'But M'am when there is a wedding, you invite all the people you know?'

'No, this is the occasion to eliminate those who do not mean much to you. Also this is the time to know those that really matter to you and to whom you matter at all. So I have shortlisted and could get less than fifty names, both friends and relatives together. They are the ones I want to be with me in jubilant times because they stayed close when I went down. They are the ones who would keep me grounded at happy times and lend me support in times of need. '

Arun looked at her and could read much more beyond her words. Yes, here was a lady, with a will of iron but with the heart as large as that of a lion. She must have seen a lot and undergone hell. Inspite of her easy smiles and vivacious deportment, she reminded him of most stoic ladies he had seen around, including his own mother, but this one was a total variant and stood out. He could not figure out what made her different or gave her the majestic bearing.

The boy shook himself up and proceeded to carry out her instructions. He brilliantly curled up the last word in each line and gave the entire write up a flighty look.

'Excellent! This is what I was looking for.' She clapped her hands with a child's mirth.

They both discussed the finer aspects pleasantly for ten minutes. All the while her eyes kept darting towards the two young people. They were lost in a deep discussion. Mili held about eight to ten cards in her hands and Abi was patiently talking and putting back the cards one by one on the shelf. Finally they came to where she was. He was holding up the card they had finally selected and taking one look at it, Shree burst out laughing and held her choice up, which was the same as the one he extended. For a minute, the two youngsters went quiet and suddenly both started laughing...he in his usual thunderous roar and Mili her girly giggles. The three were uncontrollable and didn't care about the bewildered looks of the others in the vicinity.

'So, we need to come back to my choice,' Mili chuckled happily.

'That despicable purple one? Forget it, I'll call off the wedding rather than extend such a card to people,' Abi was sharp to react.

'How dare! Are you planning to ditch me?'

'Hey cool baby, who is talking about ditching? Let's just get into a live-in arrangement. You can move in any time and of course, your mother-in-law won't mind. Of late, I keep hearing her rave about the superiority of a committed relationship over a ritualistic marriage sans commitment. ' He grinned at both of them.

'Can't you both stay serious for long? Plus, I don't become a mother-in-law unless and until you both are married. So no change of plans, mind you,' Shree tried to sound emphatic.

Mili suddenly looked ill at ease. 'Ma... I just suggested that we finalise the other card which Abi also liked, but he keeps harping on that pink card I took first.'

They had not noticed Abi move fast, quietly, back to a particular shelf, and extract a card he had replaced minutes ago.

'I see, let me check; if both of you like it then you should go for it', Shree was struggling to maintain a casual tone.

'Like this?' Mili's eyes brightened on seeing the card in Abi's hand. 'Any way we both selected it without any big dispute, for a change,' she added.

'That settles it then.' One look at the card, Shree knew that Abi would not have been too happy with it. It was very pretty indeed, with an embossed peacock feather and a golden flute on a maroon background, yet she was pretty sure that Abi would not have gone for it. Suddenly she was filled with a sense of pride. He would make a caring and loving husband unlike…

'M'am, how about words for this card? Sir said that you are going to write them too,' Arun brought her back to the present.

'Yes it's in that other file, let me show you. Find out how they want it and check out with them if there is to be any change. I need to go, and they both will tell you everything else.'

Abi walked with her to the entrance and asked, 'Are you sure you will do it alone?'

'Don't worry, my cab is waiting and the senior advocate will be in the office in another fifteen minutes. I just checked. I'll manage, see you! Have a nice time, both of you!' Shree waved to Mili and stepped out.

PART II
THE FLOW

1

The Rapids

'I just don't know how you are going to manage, but don't expect me to back you', *Amma* was furious and went on and on. 'You don't conform with anything, nor do you behave like any of those girls around you. Always your reckless attitude has landed us in embarrassing situations...',

Don't include anyone else, say 'me' and not us', Gina interjected. 'Who is that other one? Probably your mil (mother-in-law), yes I know she has been nagging you over a nonexistent issue regarding the length of my shirt and you take it out on me, right?'

'No, don't simply assume. She does not talk about your dress anymore.'

'Obviously not, after I pointed out that she is the one exposing her legs in spite of wrapping around nine yards of cloth,' Gina chuckled. 'May be, this time it is about not oiling my long flowing lovely hair'.

Gina had always felt proud of her thick long tresses and would not let anyone touch it any more, lest it should get oiled and platted tight with a ribbon tied to it. She just bound it with a simple hair-band at her nape. Her tresses were so thick that even the biggest hair clip would break when she tried to clasp it round. Of course, she had no problem styling her hair in the morning for school. Two thick plats folded in halves and tied up with two black ribbons heightened her childlike, cherubic appearance.

Her mother was now getting exasperated, 'Why are you like this Gina? Why don't you just be like the other girls in your class?' she asked in a tone that sounded more like pleading.

Gina threw a glance of disgust and disbelief, shook her head vigorously, and started moving away with the bunch of papers she was clutching in her hands.

'Why am I expected to be like any of those morons?' she muttered under her breath. About a month back, she had broached the topic of 'future plans' to a few of her classmates who were apparently closer to her. This was soon after she had decided on becoming an investigative journalist.

When she asked her friends about their plans, they were clueless as to even what they had been asked, and this baffled Gina.

'My brother has promised to send me to college but his wife wants me to stay at home and take care of the kids until they could find me a match'- this was Devi in whose household her brother, who has taken over her late father's business, was at the helm of affairs.

'My father wants to finalise my marriage as soon as I finish school', Santhi had said with a coy smile.

'My uncle's son has got a bank job and so my dad wants to perform our wedding at the earliest', Prema had said with a sense of pride.

'I will go to college and do B.A. English Literature', said Banu and Gina's eyes popped out in disbelief. Banu used to find it very difficult to understand even a nursery rhyme, leave alone the stanza from *Gitanjali*, in their English text, prescribed for memorizing.

Before anyone could ask the reason she had continued, 'My father has decided to get me a groom from Singapore and I must be able to talk some English', she even blushed, to Gina's utmost irritation.

Gina had shaken her head in despair, 'You lousy girls, all of you are hopeless! Why don't you think beyond getting married?'

The expressions of all the girls, without an exception, changed to utter disbelief and disgust.

'What are you talking, girl? When there are elders to make decisions, you are not supposed to behave and talk with total disregard for the custom. If people at home hear this we will be forbidden to talk to you', Sarasu had said in an admonishing tone.

That had been enough to blow her top. 'I disown you all! Even God cannot save you!' she got up.

'Try to save yourself first, you think a lot and read all those pillow like books from your father's collection. My mother already implied that you are going astray and...'

Before Bhagyalakshmi could finish Gina flared up, 'Enough of your sermon, conservative country cousins! You can't think for yourselves and live your lives. You have no right to pass any conviction on me. Get lost, the entire lot of you. I am ashamed of you all.'

That had got Banu irritated, 'Look at you, with all your weirdness and we have allowed you into our circle and treated you as our good friend. No one else will even want to talk to you,' she quipped.

Gina had got up with a look of abhorrence and, without a word, walked away. From then on, she had kept away from her limited group of friends. They all had tried to patch up with her, for, everyone of them loved the child in her; but they finally understood that the child had got hurt and was lost to them and then they finally had stopped bothering her. Yet, every one of them secretly yearned to resume the lively chats, whence Gina would enthral them all with fascinating stories and interesting pieces of information spiced through her own ingenious rendition.

She shook herself out of her reverie and focused on the problem at hand. All the answer scripts of her mid-term exam required her father's signature. They must be re-submitted the next day, duly signed by the parent. The previous time she could coax her mother into signing them.

When *Amma* had hesitated stating that everyone else got the father's signature, Gina had encouraged her mother, 'But those mothers are not so accomplished like you, *ma*. You are convent-educated, cultured and speak English as a native. So my class teacher will not object to it'.

Appa had been away in Surat at that time on some official work. He was a scientist in a research institute and headed a division researching on solar cells. So, he would travel once in a way to address unusual problems in the installation process. That had been the reason why *Amma* was emboldened to sign as 'the parent' then. But, now it was altogether a different story!

She peeped into *Appa*'s den. He was reading a book. He always kept the book open on the floor close to his cot, which was low, and would assume the weirdest position to read it. He would lie on his stomach upon the bed, with a pillow to support his chest, and with his head and hands hanging down read the book from above. Sometimes he would use one or two pillows beneath the book to prop it up and adjust the distance between his eyes and the book. The record player was on and Gina could make out the composition. It was Dvorak's *New World Symphony* and Gina forgot the mission at hand. The last movement was playing and she always felt that it was the best part of the composition with all the grandeur culminating into an imposing crescendo.

Appa could feel her presence but did not look up from the book. She was lost in the music stood rooted leaning on the table that stationed the record player and was very quiet. It was just one of those magic moments father and daughter used to enjoy and felt connected at a different level. The music came to a great halt with the grand finale and she had already dissolved into it.

'Gina... Gina'... 'Ginaaaa...,' *Appa* was calling from far away.

'Ha, yes *pa*', she landed aplomb.

'Why don't you change the record? Play something light,' he said without looking up from the book.

She chose Bizet from the neatly stacked pile of PVC records, replaced Dvorak back in the stack and played the *Carman Suite.*

She hunted for her papers, which she had strewn near the player, saw her father's pen nearby and picked it too. She amassed courage and sat on the floor next to the pillow that harboured the book. She was praying that her father would look up and at the same time dreading the forthcoming encounter. She felt a movement near the door and casting a sideways glance saw *Amma* moving the curtain a bit and peeping in and immediately withdrawing on catching Gina's eyes, to her utmost irritation.

Gina shuffled restlessly and finally *Appa* looked up knitting his eyebrows. He saw his pen thrust towards him followed by the bunch of Gina's answer scripts.

The Mathematics paper was on top. Originally she had kept it at the bottom but somehow she had made a blunder by not checking when she collected them back from *Appa*'s table. When *Appa* saw the red colour 35, his expression changed.

'That's out of fifty', Gina offered.

Appa went through the entire paper leisurely and looked at her with a puzzled look.

'I don't understand. You have solved all the problems and scored full marks, which, of course, totals to 35. What about the 15 marks?'

Gina swallowed hard, 'I omitted the Calculus problems. They were too vague and meaningless and I don't find any point learning the subject.'

'But everyone does, at least for the sake of marks', *Appa* looked at her now. He slowly got up and assumed a sitting posture on the bed, planting his feet firmly near the pillow.

'True *pa*. Everyone of my classmates learns the problems by heart, which I cannot do. You know, the Maths madam keeps shouting at us all the time without bothering to explain any of those steps involved and I don't like her or her subject. Algebra and Trigonometry have some logic and are not difficult to learn without her help. That's how I could score full marks in the rest of the portion'. Gina was panting now after giving a hurried explanation.

Appa signed the paper and handed it to her, just shaking his head vigorously. Next came her language paper and without bothering to check the answers or marks, he signed it. Then there was her Chemistry paper. On checking the answers, he found that she had lost marks just because none of the chemical equations was balanced.

'As long as the products are correct, why should I worry about the number of molecules?' She muttered under her breath and *Appa* shook his head again in exasperation. He just signed the next papers too.

Finally, her English paper was in his hands.

'So, is this 67% the highest in your class?' he skimmed through the script.

'No, *Appa*, Bhagyalakshmi got 84%. She exactly reproduced the notes dictated in the class. In fact Ma'm was very angry with me and asked me whether I was trying to show off. When I know the stuff, why should I memorise?'

Appa was busy writing something in the front page on top. He drew a rectangular border enclosing his text and signed beneath. Gina grabbed the papers thrust towards her and rushed out.

'Gina,' *Appa* called as she stepped out of the room. Looking back, she found him extending his hand holding the pen, 'Could you please replace my pen?'

It was done in a jiffy and going into her room she started reading *Appa*'s note to her English teacher.

'Dear Madam, 'Avuncular, nonchalant, trepidation, incredulously and verbose'- These are the words scored off by you in the first three pages even though they were aptly used- grammatically, structurally and contextually- and I also find that marks were deducted for using such words. I have not gone beyond the first three pages. Instead of discouraging students who are capable of giving original answers, I suggest, that you buy yourself a good dictionary.'

Gina couldn't control her giggles. She could visualize Suganthi ma'm's eyes popping out behind her huge glasses.

Gina, till that year, had got used to being the English teacher's pet in all classes. But Miss Suganthi's arrival that year had changed everything. She, with her M.Ed. degree, claimed to be the most qualified and experienced teacher in the whole school, and naturally she was given the best section of the highest class in the school and Gina's troubles started right from the very first class. While introducing herself Gina started, 'I am.....', Suganthi interrupted with a huge bark, 'What? You heard how everybody else introduced themselves. I will not put up with an egoist in my class. You will also fold your hands and say 'My name is so and so'. Understood? Now what's your name?'

In utter disbelief Gina had answered in a tone barely audible to herself.

'See, you don't even know how to answer such a simple question. Better know your limits and don't act smart in my class'.

Suganthi had heard about Gina before going to the class. On a casual enquiry about A-Section, all teachers in the staff room implied that it would be a pleasure teaching English to that class, especially with a student like Gina whose linguistic capacities surpassed even a post-graduate in English. Suganthi could not take it otherwise but personally, for she had always been boastful of her double post-graduation. From then on, she took every opportunity to belittle Gina and her penchant for the language. Gina was furious initially but understood that, it was Suganthi's gross inferiority complex that was freaking her out and, since then, Gina started maintaining her distance and silence.

'Try never to fight, but if you are left with no other choice, always make it a point to fight with your equals. Don't fight with small people'. *Appa* once had told her when she got angry with the servant maid, who commented on her dressing sense.

Now, what was Suganthi ma'm going to do about *Appa*'s note? She would not talk about it to the other teachers, as, by then, she had rubbed almost everyone in the staff-room on the wrong side. Nor would she dare to take it to the HM madam. She might take it out on Gina, but Gina knew that her best reaction would be to ignore Suganthi.

She realized that she had abruptly come out of *Appa*'s room, not that it was going to matter, nor would *Appa* have noticed or make an issue of such a triviality. The entire family was totally unmindful of the formalities and customary exchanges amongst themselves!

When she reached the room, she heard *Amma*'s complaining voice.

'Gina needs a bit of shaking up. She does not understand how important marks are these days.'

Appa's annoyed tone then reached her ears, 'Let her be, she is growing up into a fine young lady with a mind of her own. She is too intelligent to make sense to the people of this small place. I am happy she is uncontaminated by the stifling conservatism that prevails all around. It is not just about her, it goes for all the three of them. Don't impose anything on them. Let's give them the best of exposure and a wide berth. Just wait and watch! All our relations- I mean from both our sides- some of whom now jeer at them- will understand that these three children are much refined in their taste and are more cultured and intellectually far superior, beyond their presumptions and perceptions.'

Gina stepped into the room. *Appa* sternly looked at her and said, 'Gina, you can't afford to play the fool anymore. I am very unhappy about your performance. You must take your studies a bit more seriously.'

Gina had not expected this and was crest fallen. *Amma*'s expression said, 'See, didn't I tell you?' Gina found her attitude very irritating and mean. Of late, *Amma* had started picking too many holes as far as Gina was concerned and seem to despise the amicability that had started pervading in all dealings between father and daughter. Previously, *Appa* had also been very judgmental about her and was too difficult to please. He would never talk of the 95% she would have scored but blew up the lost 5% to an enormous disproportionate issue and made her feel very guilty, worthless and ashamed. At times Gina even suspected that he would totally disown her over a trivial issue some day.

What Gina could never understand was why she had to bear the brunt always just because she happened to be the eldest. Her sister enjoyed the immunity from *Appa*'s wrath through the protective concern of her mom and her brother being the only son, that too the youngest, was the apple of her eyes. So it was always Gina when something turned out to be other than her expectations.

Silently, she beat a hasty retreat with a sense of resentment against her mother, which was not for the first time. Why should she always spoil things between her and father? She could not help recalling the fleeting bliss of those magical moments she had shared with her dad just about ten minutes back, when she got lost in the music from the little box.

2

Still waters

'Ranjaniii……….. where have you gone suddenly? See, Raju is waiting at the table and the *dosa* pan is real hot. Should you disappear every now and then to stand in front of the mirror of yours to put on a fresh coat of lipstick', the old woman was yelling at the top of her voice and Ranjani immediately knew that it was just one of her proxies to gain the sympathy of the neighbours.

Ranjani had just gotten Raju out of bed with great difficulty and could hear him roar inside the bathroom. Disgusting swine! Mother and son made an unholy combination and would chew her head off, but as ever, she chose to ignore them completely. They did not belong in her world. She combed her wet hair and nonchalantly threw the bunch of hair that came with the comb, into the trash bin. She was a little surprised at her own insipid attitude. Her thick black hair had lost its luster and become thinner and she had cut it shorter not for any enhancement in looks but for easy manageability.

She came out of her room, went into the kitchen and started making a *dosa*. Her mother-in-law snooped from behind and started again in a hushed voice, 'He is not going to be ready in the next fifteen minutes. Are you going to serve cold *dosas* to my son?'

'That's for me', Ranjani took it off the pan and loaded it on her plate. In any case, Raju preferred to be served by the cook.

'Won't you ask about us even for a formality? With two old people and her husband, look at her indulging! No family woman would ever be so selfish and uncaring'

Ranjani left the place with just one dosa on her plate.

'What's the point?' she thought. She knew that the old couple had just finished their breakfast of the hot stuff straight from the pan, served by the cook.

Ranjani had stopped consuming anything prepared or served by that woman who called herself a cook in that house. She was yet another item added to her agenda of silent battles. That woman's audacious comments and cheeky talks, especially when Raju was around, were getting more and more nauseating and Ranjani was not a fool to miss the undertones in the casual conversations between the two of them.

Anyway, she was determined not to fight over a worthless man, with a lowly creature. She felt something tightening around her neck at the mere thought of her predicament. She started eating in silence and woke up to reality when something soft brushed her feet.

'Nila, what had you been doing all along, girl?' Absently she just took the remaining piece of *dosa* from her plate and held it for the loving bitch. Nila just grabbed it and went out to her favourite spot under the *Asoka* tree.

Ranjani dumped the plate in the sink, washed her hand and went back to her room.

She stuffed her lunch box of curd rice, which she had prepared and packed, into her handbag, looked around and found the book of *Bharathiar's* verses lying on the floor near the bed, which was a reminder of yet another of her bad nights.

Around 12-45 a.m. the previous night, after consuming a lonely dinner of cold *rotis* and *dhal* as usual, after his usual bout of brandy, Raju had walked into the bedroom and had got annoyed to see her still up and reading her book, with Pankaj Udhas singing her favourite *gazzal, Chitti ayenge* in the background.

Which one annoyed him more-the book or the music-was not evident.

'Don't you have to work tomorrow? You get up late and make mother slog in the kitchen for you.'

She was bemused and her irritation showed through her sarcastic smile.

This had made him go wild, 'Stop sniggering at me, I know what dirty thoughts are running through that stupid head of yours'.

His agitation had emboldened her, 'What am I to think of a man who can't forget his mother even in his bedroom?'

'Don't bring in your psychologist's point of view. She is everything to me. You are here on my bed because she cannot be'.

Dirty scoundrel, was he that drunk as not to even know what he had been talking or was he just vying for another argument?

Ranjani just had tried to ignore him but he wouldn't leave. As he started moving menacingly towards her, she stiffened and her huge eyes roved around looking out for something to grab and throw at him if necessary. Experience had taught him what to expect from her when cornered and hence, hesitating a little, he grabbed a dictionary from the table and threw it at her. But his coordination failed due to the quantity of liquor he had consumed and that had rendered him totally off-balance by then. The book just slipped out of his hand sideways and fell on the table again and he had slid on his side of the bed and instantly started snoring.

Ranjani was exasperated. She, by then, had geared herself up for a strong retaliation, just to remind him what to expect when she was unduly roused. That bastard would not even give her an opportunity to vent her anger. Too bad!

She had been looking for the verse about the thundering winds and lightning streaks heralding in the cool showers, by Bharathiar.

During lunch-time she was reminded of it by Dr. Venu of Tamil Department. He had taunted her and tried to extract the exact words from her and laughed at her when she failed to recall one particular word. Her gang of friends met during lunchtime, each from a different faculty and of different taste, but who came together by virtue of the common passion they all shared towards creativity and perfection. They were all devotedly involved in various activities of the college, which were projected as added-value by the management during admission time. There was also a healthy competition among her friends in equipping themselves further academically and otherwise, helping each other grow academically and intellectually. They were known as the Energetic Eight by the entire institution- some did so in awe and admiration, but most with a sense of remorse and envy.

She just had tossed the book on the table, not daring to go anywhere closer to him and it fell down on the floor, closer to the sleeping dog's side of the bed, and she decided against going there to retrieve it. Let them lie where they were- the book and the dog!

She slowly picked the book now and as she straightened, the bathroom door opened.

'How do you manage to read the verses again and again like a love letter?' this was supposed to be a joke as he gave a loud laughter and came closer, she stepped aside and said, 'I'm late already, see you later!'

There was no point in reminding him of or reviving the argument of the previous night. He would feign ignorance of any such discord and accuse her of imagining things or not being able to discriminate a dream from reality. A cunning distortive fox!

He would distort and portray any of her reminders of the rancour he spewed, as her devise to torment him in order to ensure that he would dive deep into the dire depth of destitution. The entire world believed his sweet pathetic rendition of the suffering he endured from his arrogant wife.

Further, her silence born out of her inability to talk any way but straight, would fortify his stance. Once her father had told her, 'You are too truthful and blunt and that is your strength as well as weakness.'

'Yes, truth needs no adjectives and qualifiers and is always short and crisp', she thought. 'You tend to elaborate only on what you yourself find impossible to believe.'

Ranjani ran out but remembered that she had forgotten her scooter key and returned. She froze at the door on seeing him flipping through the pages of the book she had replaced seconds ago, and focusing on the bits of papers in between the pages, on which she had scribbled whatever came to her mind at different points of time and moods.

Looking up he gave a sheepish grin, 'Came back for these? Scared that I'll find all about it?' he taunted. 'I know there is a special someone. One of these days I'm going to catch you both red handed.'

'Ya, the same way your son caught *you both* in the junk room? Don't worry! I'm still on the look-out for that elusive, real man and the moment I find him I'll make an open declaration to the entire world and plan an elopement. I will have no qualms about the whole thing. Okay, it's getting late! Will catch up in the evening! Have a great day!' she smiled sweetly at him- one of her bewitching smiles!

Ranjani moved out twirling the key in her index finger. She felt utterly happy that she had ruined his peace for the rest of the day by depriving him the pleasure of having the last word, which as far as he was concerned was his birthright as a husband.

3

Turbulance

Advocate Mithra had barely settled in his chamber when a hep-looking woman around forty years of age stood at the door with a courteous smile.

'Hope I am not late', she beamed and casually extended her hand, 'Shree!'

Suddenly the older man found himself reciprocating with such warmth that he never might have shown to any other client. His initial feeling of skepticism turned into admiration and respect. He had spoken to her over the phone and during those telecons, he had sensed that there must be something different about the person on the other end but could not exactly tell what. Now he felt everything about her was different and things were going to be very easy for him. At a closer range she appeared a little older than his first impression, but of course, he knew her real age through the data she had mailed him a couple of days back.

Normally, he found a lady-client who approached him to take up her divorce case, to be a bundle of emotions and very often there would be stormy, sentimental scenes in the chamber, much to the embarrassment of some of his young juniors and the other clients waiting in the foyer.

But, one look at Shree assured him that things would be different today. She had an air of confidence and assertiveness, which an inexperienced person would often read as signs of arrogance. A seasoned person as Mithra, with about forty plus years of standing experience in the Bar could easily read the traits.

The very brief firm handshake confirmed his perceptions and he found himself reciprocating her warm smile.

'Shree Madam, what a pleasant surprise! I was actually expecting a huge lady who would burst into tears on seeing me.'

Shree smiled as she took a seat opposite him at his large table. 'Sir, I have already sent you a twenty five paged report on what I had gone through in these twenty seven years. I find that there is no point in going over the entire thing once again.'

'Absolutely. Yet I need to ask a few questions to ascertain that this is what you really want and there would be no going back.'

'Yes sir', she leaned a little forward in all readiness.

'First, why do you want to react after twenty seven years?'

She fidgeted a little, but when she started to speak, it was in a tone of absolute clarity.

'Sir, I am not a woman devoid of empathy or sentiments. But, I cannot go on with a farce called life, just because that is what is expected of me. I was not living a life of my liking all these years. Still, I took to it since I had been under the impression that I am stuck to it and must accept it as my fate. I was expected to compromise on so many counts including my intellect and integrity, which I had been resisting all along. Every day I was fighting to survive the prevailing condition and failed to look at life beyond survival. The survival instinct always got the better of me and, suddenly, of late, I started getting the creepy feeling that I would be forced to spend the rest of my life continuing with this battle of attrition. Well, I don't know how you would take it if I said that I want to start living and stop battling, at least from this point of time.' She took a deep breath before she continued.

'I have realised that I need to be truthful only to myself and am more obliged to me than anyone else. I have started considering only myself for any major decision I would be taking in life henceforth.'

He understood her fully now and his respect and regard for her grew manifold. Here was a lady so full of life or rather the passion to live life to its fullest possible extent, with a nascent enthusiasm that would be possible only to a person who could be sincere to oneself. He saw that a tougher battle had been raging within her all along and that had literally driven her to the brink. Frantically she could make a U-turn and escape when she had almost reached the tipping point. Good for her! Not everyone could manage that.

'….. and you can even live with a sick, impoverished, illiterate, impotent idiot but not with a person who has a total lack of character and no sense of commitment…' her soft voice came drifting from a distance and he grasped the profundity of the implications of her utterance, which only corroborated his presumptions.

'Absolutely! I see you have gone through hell. But I am given to presume that you have come out unscathed. That gives an impression that you are rather insensitive. I am sorry, I am rather talking like a shrink and not an advocate. But you strike me as odd and I can't help it. Now that you are my client, you need to be very truthful, as any volte-face at a later stage would rather be embarrassing, for both of us. Moreover, this kind of demeanour would create a prejudice against you in the court room.'

She chuckled suddenly. 'I am all scarred inside. In fact the wound is still raw and accepting the same predicament as fate and expecting everyone to understand and sympathise with me will be like adding salt and chilli flakes to it. One thing, I am too proud to showcase my hurt and trepidations explicitly. Moreover, in the courtroom, I expect justice and not sympathy. Well, if the judge gets prejudiced against me, all that he could do is to reduce the quantum of settlement. Any way I am forfeiting my every claim to alimony.'

'What? Why?' he could not believe his ears.

'I hate to fix a value to what I have lost in these twenty seven years. It is too precious; it's my life, free-will, my real identity. By breaking away, I am going to get back all these intact and that matters more to me than anything else in this world.'

Mithra was totally taken aback by her blatant declaration.

'You mean, you expect nothing out of this legal separation', he could not mask his utter disbelief.

Once again she smiled gently and now he understood that it was her second nature- the smile.

'Are you sure?'

'Cent percent', her reply was crisp.

'But, madam, you need to be compensated for everything you have lost.'

'Well sir, I'm getting back my entire life. The golden opportunity to start living my life! What else would I need?'

Mithra was relentless. 'In terms of time you are twenty seven years ahead. Obviously you can't start from twenty seven years before.'

'True, but living is that which happens inside your head and cannot be reduced to temporal and spatial dimensions alone. May be, I might have missed my quota of happiness and pleasant experiences. But I could do without them and fend for myself. Probably, this ability of mine has made me what I am today, self-reliant, self-motivated and self-sufficient. A happy married life would have sucked really, given the way I see things. The monotony would have killed me but battling on a day-to-day basis has made me stronger and more enthusiastic about life. There is a perpetual quest in me to know life and what it would be offering me finally, thereby, allowing me to embrace it wholeheartedly and thus deriving a reason to live!'

Mithra once again looked at her, his disbelief and admiration growing stronger in him. He slowly removed his glasses and rubbed his forehead with his palm.

Finally, he cleared his throat and spoke, 'Then, madam, I see no problem in getting your husband to agree to file a divorce petition on mutual consent.'

Mithra was too sharp not to miss her wince at the word 'husband', which she cleverly masked with her smile, seconds later.

'Don't be so sure, sir, he would do anything to kill my happiness.'

He was taken aback. 'Anyway you have not been living under the same roof for quite sometimes.'

'Yes, for the past two years- technically speaking, but almost fifteen years to tell the truth. But he wouldn't let go of me because, he needs to inflict some kind of pain on me time and again to be assured of his hold on me. Moreover he has taken it upon himself to break me and shatter my spirit because he knows I am too good for him.'

'Anyway I will talk to him this evening and let you know. Let's hope for the best.'

He called sharp at eight. 'Madam, you were right. I have never seen a circuitous person as your... er... When I told him that you expect nothing but a divorce, he retaliated saying he would give anything other than that. My God! The way he was gloating over his absolute control over his family, which, I can see is nonexistent, I have never seen a bigger fool, not wanting to let go, just to look great in the eyes of others! Finally, I had to tell him that you would otherwise implicate him and his entire family under the Domestic Violence Act and ensure that they are behind the bars and you have all evidence and reasons to do it. Only then he has relented a little.'

Shree relaxed. 'Thank you very much sir. No one else could have done this. I'm really grateful.'

'Shree Madam, we have a long way to go. Stay optimistic. Anything could happen down the line, especially, when you are dealing with a person with such a warped mind and crooked thoughts, who constantly plans ways and means to browbeat every person in the vicinity.'

'Yes sir, I know that. We need to be on guard all the time. My concern is that the ensuing wedding of my son should go on without any hitch. Moreover, I am taking up a new job after the wedding in a corporate house. Hope I've not put my fingers on too many things simultaneously.' Shree was suddenly surprised at her ability to discuss other issues with such ease with the advocate, whom she had known only for a week. She felt as if she had known this sweet old man for ages.

When he replied, she could read the genuine concern in his voice. 'Don't worry Shree, God is with you. You have survived the worst, not without a reason. Life is going to be good to you from now on. You deserve your quota of peace and happiness and you will get it soon. I'll call you once I draft the petition and we can meet again to discuss the finer points. Good night.'

'Good night, sir.'

When she hung up she was surprised to feel tears running down her cheeks.

Funny! This happens only when people are nice to her.

There had been several instances when that mean bastard had tried to break her and make her cry and plead, and she had resisted him with such fiery defiance that most of the times, she found him cringe and slink away. Well, she still remembered the first time he had hit her, which was the only time. It was sudden and unexpected, just a demonstration of his brutal strength, which, he thought, would cow her.

He had been provoked because she had just ignored or laughed at his manipulative verbal tactics, refusing to be drawn into an argument. It was a tingling slap on her cheek; but her reaction to that blow was faster and least expected, even to her surprise. Amassing all her might she slapped him back instantly, more like a recoil. It was not much of a slap- was more a hard pat- but the fierceness in her demeanour and the glowering hatred in her eyes caught him unawares, that too, when viewed at such close quarters, and for a moment, he was paralysed.

'How dare, you hit your husband! What sort of a woman are you?'

'A woman who can respect only a real man! You are not man enough for me on any count, or, for that matter, no self respecting woman will have you. Probably that's why you have your picks from among those worthless females. Only a stinking creep as you, will treat his wife with reproach and disregard, instead of showing even the basic concern due to a fellow human being.'

She laughed and her glaring, challenging eyes must have terrified him. The *kajal* in her eyes was smudged she had not bothered to knot or plait her thick shampooed hair which was much longer at that time. He must have been reminded of the *Kali* image she had kept in the *pooja* room, much to the displeasure of the other family members, and that was the last time he came anywhere so close to her with malicious intentions, when he was disgruntled.

'Ji, did senior call?' She came out of her reverie at the insistent query from her son. She hadn't heard the car nor had she noticed his entry into the house.

Shree nonchalantly recited the conversation she had had with the advocate. 'By the way where is Cinderella?' she asked him.

'Uncle and aunty have started missing her now itself. Yesterday, when I met them, he remarked that she is now a days more of your daughter than theirs. I couldn't miss the hint and told Urmila that she must spend more time with her parents at least till the wedding'. He always used Mili's full name when he was in a serious mood.

'Hmmmm…, What do we have in our agenda for tomorrow. Did you call up that videographer boy again?'

Abi had been moving around and Shree could hear the clinking of glasses and with raised eyebrows turned towards him.

'Come on! You need to calm your jumpy nerves,' he thrust a glass of red wine in front of her, which she took without thinking, with a feeling of relief.

She could still remember the first time he had done this. It was a very difficult day and Shree was indeed a bundle of emotions, yet, generally feeling up-beat. She had made a very important decision, which would liberate her and change her life upside down. She was tense and restless. He had brought her to his small rented flat hoping to revive her sinking spirit.

For once, she had started venting out all pent up anger and remorse, blaming everything on herself. Abi, for the first time, had become a passive listener, allowing her to spend herself. She went on and on, emptying herself and finally had got her entire life out of her system. As ever, on that difficult night too, he had not just been a supportive son but a compassionate companion, a comforting confidante, sympathetic sibling, a perceptive pal and a protective parent- all rolled into one.

When Shree entered her most vulnerable phase, and presented a pathetic sight with tears rolling down her cheeks- something he had not realised was possible in her case- he was first shocked. He had then simply done the same thing then- poured out a glass of wine for her and she had grown enraged and bewildered when he offered it to her.

'Come on big girl! Don't act naïve! Nobody gets drunk over a glass of red wine. More over alcohol becomes a problem only to those who don't know how to drink without getting drunk. I have had my lessons from your brother and you can trust me on this.'

By then Shree had taken the glass in her hand, to her surprise, and taken a sip. 'Not bad!' She made a wry face. He laughed, to which she responded with her affectionate smile.

Then, once in a way, especially after a rough day, mother and son would settle down, she with her goblet of wine and he with his glass of scotch and start discussing things that are casual, comforting, invigorating and far removed from their realm of mundane affairs.

'Relax lady, you need to catch up with your sleep. You are obviously suffering from 'sleep debt' as *thatha* used to call it.' Shree had emptied the glass, strangely, lost deep in her own thoughts with Abi watching her intently.

The mention of her father brought in a flood of memories and she quietly walked towards her room and turned back at the door to nod good night to Abi. But he had already perched himself on the swivel chair in front of the computer table to play his favourite game of *Assassin's Creed series.* He was not wearing the pair of huge head-phones, which was lying on the table. He was making use of the large TV screen mounted on the wall as the monitor and this and the home-theatre speakers had rendered grandeur to the game.

He did things in style, always!

With her usual smile, she went into her room and gently closed the door and latched it up. She adjusted the volume of the speakers and softly played a Beethoven Concerto on her gadget and prepared to retire for the night. Tomorrow would be a hectic day and so would be the day after and the one after... With a yearning to finally let go and relax, she slowly closed her eyes and succumbed to her usual shallow slumber.

PART III

RESPITE

1

Make me sing!

All the three of them were waiting at the small railway station, which had just two tracks and a single platform open to the blue sky. Gina was totally oblivious of her surroundings and her restless mind was camouflaged by her still form, as she perched on the back rest of the cement bench, firmly planting her feet on the seat. Her sister, Jayji, was sitting on the bench next to her feet, humming a song, and her brother Dippy was clinging to the areal roots of the banyan tree and trying to swing. They were there to welcome their father who had been away in Assam for almost a month. He must have reached Madras, the day before and would have taken the express train the previous night as per his original plan. Those were the days when people never even thought of the possibility of a gadget like the mobile phone and they had to rely on the postal department for any form of communication.

She saw the station-master walking in their direction and her face brightened as she recognised him to be her classmate Gowri's father.

He gave her a gentle smile and in a patronizing tone asked, 'So, you are waiting for your father, all the three of you, right? The train is running late as usual. But it will reach in another ten minutes.' He kept walking past them. She saw the big bamboo ring, which looked like a huge racquet without the frets and the folded green and red flags in his hands. She loved to watch the exchange of the bamboo rings between the loco-pilot and the stationmaster, the former would throw it on the platform a little before the engine reached the spot where the station-master stood and hook the ring extended by the latter, into his hand at the elbow. Every time she felt like asking someone, as to why these two should be in such hurry to get over with the exchange process. Anyway, the train would stop there for a full two minutes and that would be ample time to go ahead with the exchange...

The distant whistle sent a thrill through her spine and she jumped on the ground and pulled her shirt lower and adjusted her reefer skirt. The black demon was now visible and was puffing towards the station after getting past the cabin at a distance. The meter-gauge track ran straight and Gina abruptly turned in the opposite side to catch a quick glimpse of the vanishing point, about which *appa* had given an interesting input sometimes back.

The loco huffed and puffed and came to a grinding halt. White steam hissed out from the side of the cylindrical part and black smoke billowed out from the top.

As she spotted her father stepping onto the platform from the third carriage, she started running like a child, simply forgetting that all eyes were on her. Somehow, Dippy managed to reach first and took the smallest bag from the smiling man's hand. As he got down, Gina noticed something blue hanging on her father's back, mostly hidden by his form. He looked at her sister and said, 'Haven't you been eating at all? You look thinner.'

At the same time, he had casually taken off the blue thing and held it out to Gina, who just took it in her hand without removing her eyes from his face darkened by the soot from the engine, and then looked at the object and gave a shriek of surprise. It was a cute guitar made of bamboo and was wrapped up in a transparent cover.

On the way back home, *Appa* was telling them all about Assam- the innocence of people, enigmatic terrain, unpredictable weather, impenetrable forests, incessant rains- with ease, he was giving a graphic description of those distant lands transporting the three spellbound children there with him, guiding them into the enticing wonderland and all along making them enjoy every moment of their rendezvous with ardent passion and avid and intense desire to enjoy those exquisite pleasures of life.

On reaching home, all the three children ran in to get ready for the day. Gina realized that she had one of those horrible tests for internal assessment, as her final semester examination was also drawing near. She plunged headlong into the harsh reality and tried to recollect the remarks of a few critics on the verses in Milton's *Paradise Lost -Book IV.* Failing in her attempt, she smiled with guile and decided to resort to her own technique, that is, write her own criticism using some high-sounding words and acknowledge them to some non-existent critics. Her lecturers who were so trusting and who had no means of checking the veracity of those quotes would succumb unwittingly to her audacious ploy.

Gina was in a state of very high restlessness bordering irritation for no reason that particular day. She was so relieved when the last hour turned out to be a free hour because of the sudden work burden on the lecturer who was supposed to teach Phonetics. 'What a relief', thought Gina who found the lecturer's artificial accent and faulty intonations very funny and irksome, throughout her class. Instead of going to the library as directed, she started walking towards the gates of her college.

The watch-man saw her approach and was puzzled. This was the sixth consecutive year he had been watching this charming but quiet girl and this was the first time that she had dared to do the prohibited thing in that prison like women's college- leave the premises before four o' clock. He remembered the bubbly girl who had come with her mother for admission to the pre-university class and had stunned him with a, 'Hello, uncle'. In all his 25 odd years at the gate, no student had so far greeted him or called him 'uncle' and that had turned him bitter and hostile towards the entire lot. He had developed an exceptional soft corner for Gina since then. She never forgot to greet him or at least wave at him with that cherubic smile of hers all these days while going through the gate. Occasionally she would stop by, and ask about her bus or something else that would be bugging her at that moment.

Gina, after her one-year pre-university course had wanted to do her graduation in Psychology. But, that small town women's college narrowed down her options and finally to appease her father's expectations that his daughter would one day become a great scientist like him, took up Physics for her graduation. To her dismay, she found that though she liked Physics, she had to put up with the robots of the Mathematics department and, also with a Chemistry professor with a highly volatile temper, who had taken a distinct dislike for Gina for no known reason. Thus, she had a miserable academic life for three years. After her disappointment with her childhood school friends, she had not got close to anyone, though, at the same time, she had not antogonised anyone.

After completing her graduation, she realised that if she stopped, her mother would try to get her married off. By then, both father and daughter had been disillusioned about the prospects of her becoming a scientist. So, this time when she mustered courage and declared that she wanted to do an M.A. in English Literature, her parents conceded.

Her avid, astute reading habit all these years had given her an edge over all her classmates, even though they all had been from an English Literature background in the under-graduation years. They realised that she was indeed a competition to reckon with. However, Gina never treated any of them as a competitor. She never failed to bestow the benefit of her literary knowledge and exposure on all of them and encouraged them to enjoy their studies. She was a pleasant companion and a good motivator. She topped the class but never allowed that to go to her head. She remained simple, down to earth, friendly with everybody but nobody's friend in particular.

The little girl who had first called the old watchman 'uncle' had now mellowed into a final year student of post graduation. Now, unlike in the case of the other girls whom he mercilessly shooed away if they tried to sneak past the gate before time, the old man felt his heart grow with concern for this girl, who had become more of a loner and sat with a book, under a favourite tree of hers during the breaks and free hours.

He opened the gate for her and gently asked, 'Not feeling well, *Paappaa?*'

'Mild head ache and no class, by the way, can I go out now itself, uncle?' She was suddenly confused with his readiness to let her out instead of tendering the usual reproachful comments he spewed on the other girls.

He gave a gentle laughter as if he had read her confused mind. '*You* can go *Paappaa*. Just walk a little faster you can catch the 3.15 bus.'

'Thanks, uncle', she beamed at him and walked past and he locked up the gate after her.

Gina was quite bewildered by the six strings in the guitar. She was trying to tune it and was clueless as to how it should be done. The first four strings now sounded like her father's Veena and she tried various notes for the other two and finally settled for something that sounded less harsh and more in-sync with the other four.

Next came the problem of holding and fingering and she settled for a position that was less straining or painful to her fingers. She tried playing *Vara veena...* and could produce marvelous results in her first attempt.

Emboldened by her initial success, she tried out a few melodies from the Hindi and Tamil movies. Yes! She could produce the desired notes and sounds but felt that something was grotesquely wrong and grossly missing. The music was totally unlike anything produced by the guitar anywhere else in the world, so she thought, and after struggling for sometimes she gave up... for the time being.

She made it a practice to give it a try every now and then, but ensured that her father was not around when she did so.

On one such occasion, as she was trying to play the opening bars of *I have a Dream*, one of her favourite *ABBA* numbers, she suddenly felt another presence near the doorway and stopping abruptly looked up. There he was with a big smile, almost appearing to be controlling his laughter, well... what was his name? She had forgotten. He had approached her father, requesting him to be his supervisor for his final year engineering project and as she brought the tea cups, her father had even introduced them and given his name, which she could not recall right now.

There he stood tall and lanky at the door, slightly tilting his head with its long hairstyle and thick sideburns, typical of boys his age and dressed in a checked bell-bottom pants and a printed shirt. His thick moustache, bent downward like *Tiga's* handlebars, rather had irritated Gina in the first instant itself.

With a bewildered look, she put the instrument on the sofa and got up. '*Appa* is not yet back from office. Please, come in.'

He coolly walked in and sat on the chair in front. 'Can I have some water, please?'

She ran into the kitchen with a relief of escaping the embarrassing moment. *Amma* was mixing up the *dosa* batter and looked up.

'Remember that Engineering student who came the other day to see *appa*? He is there and he wants water.'

'Did you tell him to come in and sit down?' You take the water from that earthen pot. It's cool. Switch on the fan. I'll mix coffee and bring it. *Appa* will be back any minute.'

When Gina re-emerged from the kitchen with a glass of water, she was surprised to see the guitar in his hands. He was tuning it and looked up. His face brightened for a fleeting moment when he saw her and in a matter of fact tone he informed, strumming the strings one by one, 'E...B...D...G...A...E.. that's how it goes with the guitar.' She was struck by the velvety quality of his voice as he hummed softly.

He was surprised to see her mouth the equivalent *swaras*, 'sa...ma...ni...ga...pa...sa...' softly. She caught him gazing at her fixedly as he sipped the cool water, and after a few silent and disturbing seconds, Gina asked, 'So you are a guitarist, right?'

He struggled to control his laughter and this greatly irritated her, 'Yes, I am, and I play the lead in a band,' for a minute she looked perplexed and then with the curiosity of a child she looked eagerly at him.

'Can you tell me something about this instrument, *Appa* got it from Assam and told me to explore and learn to play it myself, I am trying.'

He looked skeptical, 'Are you telling me that this is the first time you are playing it? Not bad, you have music in your head and can play whatever you want, with a little conscious effort.'

Once again, his patronising tone annoyed her. He must be either her age or younger by at least six months but she felt like a naïve child while talking to him.

Well, she decided to show him his place.

'I presume you will be visiting our house frequently for your project discussion with my dad. So whenever you are here, can you teach me something about the guitar? Today I have learnt how it is to be tuned and thanks a lot for that.'

'Would be my pleasure! Next time I will teach you a few major chords and you can practice. By the way, can you read staff notations?' He paused, looked into her huge eyes, which appeared almost ready to pop out and gently added, 'Don't bother! You can easily pick them on the way. You need to be at it rigorously, for that matter, any instrument becomes your loving child depending on the way you handle it, Gina...'

She thought he unnecessarily prolonged her name with a sonorous lilt and felt a little uneasy.

'Hello Raghu, sorry, I got delayed at the railway gate… so you are a guitarist… now I remember. The other day you were telling something about your band and practice. Why don't you tell Gina how to produce the right kind of noise? The minute she returns from the college, she starts, and contrary to my expectations that she would improve as days go by, the decibel level is going up every day and getting on all our nerves.' He laughed his usual guileless laughter, as he always did every time he made fun of her.

Gina was furious. He can't do this in front of a stranger who was about to formulate a somewhat good opinion about her! She just bit her fleshy lower lip and glared at her father. Raghu was too quick, quick enough to catch the brief expression of hurt in those huge eyes and gently added, 'There is music in every noise and she has a good ear for music. Already I have started the lessons, Sir.'

'Oh really? Great! Okay Raghu, just give me ten minutes to wash and change and then we can have a sitting,' he went in.

'Thanks a lot Raghu.' Having been reminded of his name, she found herself using it with ease.

Before he could say anything *Amma* came with a plate of hot *dosas* and white coconut *chutney*. 'First eat something. Once you start, you both will go on talking and forget everything. 'Gina, can you check if *appa* is ready and make his *dosas?*'

Amma had a way of ensuring that Gina was assigned some work in the kitchen every now and then and gave the usual reason for it, that a girl should be well trained. Gina always wondered why her sister was simply exempted from this general rule, not that she minded because she loved to experiment in the kitchen and more so, enjoyed assisting her father whenever he would decide to give a day off to her mom and cook exotic food items with very ordinary ingredients. Gina's preference for puddings and soups over *sambar* and *avail,* was much to her mother's displeasure. As it was, Gina was visualized as an alien in the women's realm.

Gina always had felt that not only her mother and grandmother but almost all women have a habit of making a mountain out of a mole hill, when it came to those womanly chores. They simply felt as if they were the custodians of tradition in matters concerning running the house and never could take on improvisation and ingenuity. Gina always would say that they all must have been cast in the same mould. They always criticized her artistic creation of the *Rangoli* patterns rendered without the customary dots or some gravy tried with new ingredients to bring in the desired enhancement in aroma and taste.

Once in a way, her father would take her mother on short trips, either to attend functions or just somewhere to beat her mother's monotony, leaving the house and Gina's siblings in Gina's custody. Sometimes, Gina's mother would insist on going out somewhere exactly when Gina's academic calendar was fully up with tests, assignments, projects and other activities. Any protest from Gina would draw harsh caustic remarks, born out of self-sympathy, from her mother. She would even call Gina a spoil-sport and accuse her of trying to spoil whatever little 'change' she was getting, just to spite her, as if mother and daughter were archrivals. That was mainly because she would always project her role as the lady of the house as one of martyrdom, at which Gina would split into bursts of laughter. Further, she would never miss a chance to go around boasting about her very responsible eldest daughter's capabilities to her envious relatives. So, rather than being called selfish, Gina would prefer to sacrifice a little bit of her sleep and her rendezvous with *Tiga* and music or books and do a balancing act with cooking, house-keeping and her studies as well, without complaining, unwittingly, thereby encouraging her mother to plan the next trip at the earliest opportunity.

As Gina disappeared into the kitchen, her mother started her chatter with Raghu, who was thanking her for the nice soft homely *dosas*. 'Don't be so formal Raghu, such behaviour is not warranted in this house.'

He could not make out whether her voice was tainted with pride or scorn.

But in the days to come, he would integrate into the system that prevailed in the house to such an extent that he would walk straight into the kitchen in the evenings, heartily asking, '*Mami*, what yummy thing have you made today for tiffin?'

After having his heart's fill there, chatting with her and eating all the while, he would come to the hall where Gina would be sitting with her guitar and catch up with her. He had understood that she resented anything formal even when it came to learning music. All the time she wanted to experiment and explore and incidentally pick up a certain tune or chord. He complied with her whims all the while, secretly admiring the spirited, self-willed girl, a rather strange specimen in those parts. What added to her charm was her innocence and her total oblivion of her own uniqueness and the resulting lack of arrogance or haughtiness. Sometimes he sympathized with the child, who was seeking acceptance and acknowledgement from the world around that was constantly pointing fingers at her and demanding that she behaved normal like the other girls her age.

He made it a point to come for the sessions with Mr. Prabhakar, Gina's father, at least an hour earlier than the assigned time, so that he could give sufficient time to his taste buds and her guitar.

On one particular evening, not finding Gina in her usual place, he went back to the kitchen.

'Oh, I forgot to tell you, Gina has gone to her friend's engagement ceremony. That silly girl refused to go but I somehow compelled her and sent her. It won't look nice, since these two girls had been classmates right from standard two. I don't understand this daughter of mine. She hates to attend any function and avoids being into a crowd of even known people.' She was now talking to herself and the conversation had turned into a soliloquy.

Raghu slowly walked back into the hall and opened his note-book and took back to the pencil sketch he started the previous night. Suddenly he felt empty, with his enthusiasm totally drained. Time stood still and his mind was seeking that which he was agonizing over. He knew that it was not meant to be, but could not help yearning for the elusive impulse. His inner voice chided him and warned him. It was pulling him back and holding him right there and he dared not venture beyond that foreboding, invisible line.

Time started ticking again and he did not realize that his meticulous work had taken him deep into almost one hour. Suddenly he felt a shadowy presence and inhaled a whiff of some exotic perfume nearby, and looking up, he was stunned.

It was Gina, looking totally unlike herself. There she was, draped in a pale pink sari and wearing a strand of pearls round her neck and a set of matching pair of ear-drops. The fragrance of the long string of jasmines that adorned her loosely platted thick black hair wafted past his nostrils.

Raghu looked up into her eyes and got lost! She held a finger against her lips and was cautioning someone at the front door, which was behind Raghu, to be silent, and the mischievous smile and the sparkling eyes mesmerised him. Slowly turning around, he found her father stopping midway in his attempt to say something and looking at him.

He felt the notebook snatched out of his hands in a jiffy, and Gina held it in front of her father for his scrutiny, all the while not taking her eyes off it. He tried to cover up his embarrassment and mumbled, 'I was just waiting for you and…'

'That is *appa*'s favourite posture and expression. So brilliant. *Appa* this is what you look like while you play the *veena*', she giggled and it became a hearty laughter.

Raghu had sketched Mr. Prabhakar with his *veena* across his lap, in his usual one leg-folded posture. The eyes were half closed and he could be seen enjoying the music he produced.

'That's a good one. Can I have it?' he asked Raghu.

Raghu looked confounded and was dumb-struck. He just nodded.

Appa looked at her mother, who emerged into the hall and simply said, 'While coming from the office I suddenly remembered that Sethu had invited me to his daughter's engagement. You know whom I saw there? This big baby of ours, with the bemused expression of a lost child, a total misfit in that atmosphere. Why do you do this to her? I heard the argument between the two of you this morning- she, refusing to go and you, forcing her- why are you so cruel to her? Once the function got over, I brought her along. Both of us are very hungry and you better feed us first. Raghu, what's for dinner today?'

Her mother's expression changed to one of intense animosity. 'Excellent! Who would attend a function and rush back home for dinner without eating anything there, excepting the two weird people here?' She smiled at Raghu as if seeking his support and followed her husband into their room.

She was curious to know more about the function- who else had been there and all other details regarding the impending wedding- not just the date, how much dowry would be given and how many sovereigns of gold the bride would get and what were the other terms and conditions involved in the marriage. She knew that Gina would not have bothered to find out all these and any query would elicit an explosive response from her. Even Gina's father would not have bothered about knowing all these details but a casual conversation he must have had at the function would have equipped him with the required data, unwittingly!

Gina shifted her gaze from her parents' direction to the paper on the ground that had dropped from the notebook when she snatched it from Raghu's hands. Raghu was simply stumped by the new bewitching look of Gina- totally unlike her tomboyish self- with her grace and poise that had just banished the overgrown child he had known all along.

May be, this was the moment he had been waiting for; the yearning in him grew stronger and irrepressible. He was on the verge of making a long cherished confession- the real reason behind his association with her father. He was anxious to get everything out of his system and he made a desperate attempt to give expression to his overwhelming emotions.

He had not noticed the paper he had preserved for the past so many years slip out of his notebook and fall beside his feet on the floor. The paper was more yellowish and must have been five or six years older than the notebook. Noticing that it was yet another pencil sketch, Gina dived for it and took it in her hands. It was only then that Raghu realised that it had flown to the ground and he just stood there paralysed. The sketch on it showed a very young girl sitting at a waterfront and the sky and the surroundings were dotted with birds of different forms. There was a huge tree near the girl and she was engrossed in something that she was writing in a book she had on her knees.

Everything about the picture was familiar to her including the dress the girl was wearing and the patterns on her shirt, yet she could not put her finger exactly into it. She peered into Raghu's eyes as if demanding an explanation.

'That is the image of an angel who came in my dreams when I was young. I think, I was in class eleven when I made it.' He tried to sound normal but his voice faltered in his anguish to mask the truth of the matter.

'Do you know her. Is she your friend?'

'That girl? Oh no! I Just used to catch a glimpse of her, once in a way, most of the times in my dreams.'

'What is she writing, a love letter to you?' she rendered lighter veins to the moment and giggled. The child was back!

'I don't think so. She is too serious minded for that. May be she is writing a poem or solving a puzzle.' Raghu heaved a big sigh of relief to note that she had been deluded.

'Do you still dream of her?'

'No. There is no need and time for dreams right present. The *reality* is more interesting *now*.' Stopping suddenly, he looked at her again and got lost into those huge eyes.

Gina disentangled her gaze from his with ease. It was more like slithering out of his eyes, and she slowly moved towards her room with an inscrutable glazed look.

'Gina...', his voice was a mere whisper. He was literally choking on his own consuming feelings. Again, she turned around in response with a twinkle in her eyes that flashed just momentarily and disappeared along with her smile of mirth. Her momentary confusion, bordering on wonder made her dumbstruck and she wanted to hear him again.

Time stood still and Raghu felt the overpowering restraint taking hold of him once again. Totally bereft of those nascent passions, he found his voice faltering and it was a mere whisper, 'Gina..., I just thought of...'

Gina stood facing him, her head tilted to a side and her eyes boldly engaging his. Her smile reappeared, 'Yes, Raghu, even I missed.'

'What?' he was barely audible.

'Our session today! I am so sorry about it.'

'Why?' He sounded calmer even though his heart was racing.

Now her confusion was visible and she went still again.

'Gina, when I didn't find you, I realised how much I miss...'

'...the guitar, right?' she completed for him.

'May be. It has made a difference...'

Gina looked at him intently with a flicker of smile on her face, waiting for him to complete.

He abruptly stopped and strained visibly to check his over-brimming emotions. Finally, with an effort, he smiled at her and simply said, 'I could not recognise you in this sari for a second. You look good. More like a lady!'

'Oh, thanks! Can we catch up tomorrow? Have to complete an assignment! See you!' She simply waved at him, turned around, walked and disappeared into her room, closing the door gently behind her.

Raghu was staring at her closed door, his anguish writ all over his face. He cursed himself under his breath. 'No, it can't be! It shouldn't be.' He shook his head vigorously and went out of the house almost in a run. He reached the bamboo gate and stopped clinging to it. His entire frame was shaking in a spasm of sobs and not able to withhold any longer he cried out in pain, 'Ginaaaa…..', and his voice got drowned in the opening bars of some concert that emanated from within the house.

Raghu's sessions with Mr. Prabhakar came to an abrupt end, when his project work got ready for submission.

The evening before, he had come for one last session to seek Mr. Prabhakar's signature in the bound volumes and more importantly, his blessings. He was given a great grand dinner in their home. The short association of two months filled him with awe for the entire family. Jayji had been home from the college hostel for her study holidays and he met her for the first time. She was pursuing her second year Computer Engineering Course in the city college and hence had to stay in the hostel. Dippy, now a class twelve student, was, for a change, free of his tuition classes and stayed at home for dinner. He had been maintaining a very cordial relationship with Raghu, and sought his guidance regarding college admissions and other such matters for the years to come.

During dinner in the open terrace, in the diffused moonlight, they were just chattering and for the first time he was simply amazed at the smartness of the children and their ability to discuss a wide variety of topics and when he openly marvelled at it, Mr. Prabhakar casually informed him, 'We follow certain rules for our discussions. Talking about people around and talking about mundane incidents like, how one missed the bus and managed to reach the exam hall on time are taboos. Otherwise they can talk about anything under the sun.'

'Sitting under the moon,' Gina added with her mouth full of *semiya payasam.*

'Gina, behave like a lady', her father reminded her of her forgotten manners gently.

She was already busy loading her cup with a second helping of the sweet dish. The entire family had very special kind of 'sweet-tooth'. They all had the habit of searching for some sweet, at least a piece of jaggary, after a hearty meal.

After three hours of laughter, banter and some serious discussions, Raghu started to say 'bye' to those amazing people around. Finally, he came to Gina, who was standing a little away from the others, holding on to the parapet wall and peering at the full moon through the mango leaves that blocked her vision. When he looked at her, he felt his chest tighten and moving a bit closer he held out his hand. As she took it, he simply said, 'Don't abandon your guitar. You have lots of sweet music in you.'

Gina suddenly grew quiet and tense. She tried to say something but just smiled and looked up. She could see his eyes gleaming in the moonlight and suddenly remembered the pencil sketch of the girl, which he had made long back.

She opened her mouth as if to make a query but immediately held herself back, yet he could sense the unasked question in her eyes. Raghu just held her gaze and waited for an eon.

'Do you still dream of her?' she asked suddenly and softly, breaking that awkward silence that pervaded their time and space.

He was jolted out, since he was right then recalling her innocent queries on seeing the sketch a month ago.

'No, may be, I'll resume my dreams soon.'

She did not ask anything more.

'All the best', she said lightly.

'Thanks Gina, you too take care. You are a very special person. May be, you are not aware of it yourself. Keep yourself intact. Don't lose your liveliness in the course of your life! All the best!' He abruptly turned away and walked down the steps.

It was a difficult moment indeed, and all along he had been anticipating and dreading it. He felt he had managed it with ease, yet was not sure. A part of him rebelled, imploring him to go back to make a declaration. At the same time an inner voice goaded him to move on. His anguish prolonged his casual descent down the stairs. He could feel Gina moving slowly and following him but she stopped as soon as she reached the top of the stairs. Suddenly, he stopped and turned up as he reached the landing and with a great effort repeated, 'Take care, Gina!'

Gina slowly came out of her daze and looked around. Her mother and sister had cleared the plates and vessels and were stacking them to be taken down stairs. Her father was pointing to the star *Antaris* in the constellation of *Scorpio* to her brother and telling him how the ancient Indian astronomers had named that biggest of the visible stars very aptly as *Jeshta Nakshthra,* meaning 'big brother star'. Gina joined them.

The sky above had always fascinated her and she would spend hours together peering into the clear sky during summer months. With her father's guidance and using the star atlas in their library, she could identify most of the visible constellations, and also recognise their *Alpha* and *Beta* stars by name. She could even tell the *Nakshathra* of the day according to the Indian system of astrology, just by looking at the moon's proximity to a particular star in the zodiac constellations. Her mother sometimes mocked at her habit of going to the terrace on most of the clear nights for star-gazing and would comment that she had to take attendance like a nursery school teacher, lest one of the star pupils should run away and play truant.

Raghu had now gone to the back of her mind and she didn't realize then that it was the first step out of her mind. They had not yet become fast friends, as far as she was concerned, but he was definitely more than just an acquaintance. At times she had been disturbed by his long silent gazes during their guitar sessions, but never gave any serious thought to it. He would appear to be on the verge of making some kind of confession and when she raised her brows as if asking him to come clean, he would shake his head with a silly grin and she would wonder if he was trying to repress a sarcastic comment about her skills at the guitar.

When she finally came down, she remembered that the next day was to be her last day in college, as they were at the fag end of that semester and the study holidays, the last of its kind for her, would then commence.

Suddenly, she also remembered that there was a farewell party the next day given by her juniors. She was the most favourite *akka* for all the UG and PG girls pursuing English literature course. She had also promised that she would sing a nice song for them and started wondering which one that would be!

2

I sing your song!

'**D**on't forget the reception in the evening. I have promised Mahesh that you would attend it.' Raju was shouting after her.

Ranjani stopped her scooter and turned her head with such a fury that he was taken aback by her defiant look. The boy sitting on the pillion almost got thrown off and held her shoulders to steady himself.

'Didn't I make it clear last night that I can't be dragged along to please the whims and fancies of all and sundry. By the way, who is this Mahesh and why should I attend his sister's wedding reception without an invitation?'

'You will do so because you are my wife and because I say so...'

She got exasperated and seeing the old woman rushing out to her son's aid, she hurriedly ended the argument. 'Okay, but he will come along too,' she pointed to their son, who was adjusting himself on the pillion of her scooter, totally oblivious of the roaring argument and the raging temper.

'Why should you drag me along,' he asked her with all remorse when they swapped seats after the scooter turned the corner. A fourteen year old was not supposed to drive yet, but he felt fully responsible for his mother and had started taking it on himself to render a physical and emotional shield for her. Sometimes he was over-protective and frequently would shoo away his abusive father with just a glare. He had inherited her huge eyes and sweet smile, which gave him a handsome and mature look.

'You will know it in the evening', she calmly replied.

The three of them presented the perfect sight of a happy family, with Ranjani walking between her husband and son with her charming smile through the introductions. Raju stayed with them for about five minutes ensuring that they both sat in a corner close to the dais on which a band was playing old and new numbers in all languages. The backdrop showed a rounded tree and glittering letters that read '*UTHAM BAND*'.

The lawn, on which the reception was held, was beautifully lit and the music was soft. In a tone faked with redundant concern and in a voice audible above the band to most people around, he looked at her and said, 'You will enjoy the music. I'll meet a couple of my friends and be back in a jiffy. You just relax.' With these words he just turned and walked away fast.

She knew what would follow in the next hours. This was not the first experience of its kind. He would disappear with a few other men and be back- only after the band had disbanded- completely inebriated, and make her drive the car back home.

With a sigh, she just sat and turned towards her juvenile escort. He gave a mischievous smile.

'I'm going to the dining hall, coming?'

She glared at him and he quietly slipped away. She just looked on. It was very pleasant indeed and she slowly dissolved into the music. The band had two guitarists, a keyboard player, a percussionist and a couple of singers. All of them were singing along with two main singers, especially, those lines meant for chorus and had been producing an overall good effect. She was sitting like a statue, with her raving mind roving in all directions. She presented a perfect picture of a calm and composed lady, at peace with herself and the world around, but people who knew her well would read the turmoil that went inside her being, and her frantic struggle to silence everything.

When the lead guitarist started off with the opening notes of her favourite song of yester years, a thrill ran through her form.

'Chiquitita tell me what's wrong...' He was also mouthing the words along and she looked up.

He was watching her and strumming the guitar. His clean shaven face, short haircut with a bunch of hair falling on his face and intent eyes gave him the look of a pathetic poodle. She felt that he was singing for her. The song brought in floods of memories, which looked like those from her distant past.

Why should he sing the song as if to remind her that she was a loser. Yes! She was indeed one! Having lost her life, battling to save herself- from what?

What more is there to salvage? She was caught in a vicious circle.

Breaking away would be very easy, but to what effect? It might fetch her the kind of freedom that would be restricting.

Breaking away would leave her all by herself and it would be even more difficult to come out of that vacuum that she would then get trapped into.

She would have to let go everything and no one would understand her stance. Raju had taken extensive care to project himself as a perfect family man- a doting husband and a loving father. On the contrary, Ranjani had been viewed as an insensitive woman, who would say and do things, unmindful of the hurt inflicted on her dear husband. Thanks to his manipulative deceit in showing off his nonexistent concern for her when he had an audience!

She knew that like a dumbo she had been putting up with more than she should.

Nothing worse could happen to her, nor could she hope for anything better by breaking free.

May be she would get a freedom which would be of no use to her but further tether her to sentiments and guilt.

'…try once more like you did before sing a new song chiquitita'

The song ended at last and she felt herself being rudely shaken and a cup with a double scoop of ice-cream thrust before her. 'I got this for you. I know you are not going to eat anything here and I had no intentions of starving. Your wonderful husband may not be back in another hour.'

She was irritated by his remark, 'Call him you loving father instead', she quipped.

But he was gone. She saw him talk to one of the singers, obviously requesting a song, and when that was conveyed to the rest of the band, she could feel the electrifying excitement that ran through the six people on stage. Probably their current favourite too, and she immediately understood the reason when the song started- *'Have you ever really loved a woman?'*

Ranjani glanced at her son, who now occupied the seat next to hers.

With a mischievous smile she asked, 'Have you?' She was more relaxed now. May be, it was the band or the vicinity of her son or most probably the combined effect.

He retaliated with unexpected ire. 'I do have a lot of friends who are girls but not a single girl friend, nor will I ever have one. I have no faith in marriage or for that matter any relationship.'

She was stunned by his open animosity. She decided to ignore this attitude for the time being. The poor boy had been exposed to what a relationship was not supposed to be. He would grow out of it, given some time.

His hostility to his father was developing multi-fold and would manifested at the least expected times. She had downloaded a few poems of Sylvia Plath and stored the collection in the desktop of their computer. The entire collection, especially *Daddy,* had elicited great admiration from the boy. The abusive terms and imagery had enthralled him and one evening when he accompanied her and Nila in their usual walk, he started a discussion on it. She was bewildered by his show of such intense hatred for his father and all her attempts to gloss over the situation at home made him more explosive.

He simply said, 'My daddy is a stinker, a rotten toe in a century old, unwashed socks.'

She was shocked to hear him recite the most formidable line of the poem, *'Daddy, daddy, you bastard, I am through.* Ha ha... I really like the last line.'

'Shut up, will you?' she flared up.

'Ha ha... feeling angry? Can you? You are an inert idiot and you refuse to take the reins of your life in your own hands, under some clumsy notions and excuses.' He tried to provoke her further but she ended the conversation with her silence.

The band played on and she lost count of the minutes that ticked by. She could see that Nandhu was also enjoying the music and once in a way he was approaching the stage with some request, mostly her favourites from the Tamil and Hindi movies of the seventies.

He slowly leaned towards her and whispered in her ears, 'Ranji, that joker is back and has been trying to get our attention for the past ten minutes. He is near the entrance. At least he has the decency not to enter the place when fully drunk! Don't turn that way for sometimes. Let him get desperate.' He was giggling uncontrollably. She joined and turning towards the stage, she caught the guitarist giving her an inscrutable stare, which reminded her of something or someone. Before she could sort out her confusion, she smelt Raju very close.

'How could you both totally forget me? It's not that easy to get rid of me, you both will then end up out in the streets.' He was gradually getting louder and both of them simply got up and walked past him towards the entrance and to the parking lot to escape those familiar embarrassing moments.

'So, you did have a good time!'

No! Ranjani was not going to take the bait and ignored the remark, which she knew was a barbed query; but her husband was not going to leave her in peace. He seemed to have come prepared with a set plan for the night.

Their son had gone into his room and banged the door shut, making his fury evident, as soon as they reached home. Ranjani changed her silk sari and took the jewelry and jasmine strand off her presence and got ready for bed when he tried to force the conversation.

'Won't you even bother about making some dinner for me?'

'I'm tired and sleepy and tomorrow is a working day. Your mother is in charge of your house and the kitchen and I have no obligation or right as far as you are concerned. Moreover, I know that you had got some stuff from some cheap roadside eatery because the car was reeking of spices and we had to roll down the glasses on the way back. Let me go to bed. Good night.' She moved away towards the bed but he was there right in front, covering the distance in a couple of bounds.

'What are you trying to hide? You think I didn't notice? What a shameless creature, flirting with strangers and using her own son as a messenger.'

She knew that it was his guilt feeling and inferiority complex again. Any retaliation would aggravate the situation, as he was inebriated; further the fighter in her was thoroughly exhausted. She could not comprehend the new story he was cooking up, which would be, anyway, transmitted to his mother in the morning and subsequently relayed to his sisters over the phone.

Slowly the story unfolded to her amazement. 'So it is that Utham guy this time. He was eating you up with his staring eyes and you were shamelessly tapping your feet for every note he played on that stupid instrument he was flaunting round his neck. How did you get to know that he still is an eligible bachelor with an MBA from an IIM and holding some position in an MNC and like most of you fools he also goes around telling music is his passion?'

'So, that was his name, Utham? Thanks for the update. Let me sleep. I'm tired'. She manoeuvred past him carefully, so careful that not even the edge of her rustling dress would come in contact with his person and sat reclining on the left side edge of the bed.

But the beast would not leave her at it and hence she switched off her senses and sank into an oblivion. Slowly she stretched herself and covered her body from head to toe with the thin blanket she had kept especially for such occasions. Practice had made it easier for her to distance herself from the situation and float into some balmy, distant realm filled with sweet memories and fond voices, through the velvety darkness inside the cover. Raju's insistent droning failed to reach her and ultimately he had to give up.

He was furious and frustrated at his consistent failure to inflict any kind of pain on her anymore.

Initially, her frightened form excited him more than anything else. When he had sensed that all she could give him was contempt and disdain, he decided to punish her until she begged him to stop and fall at his feet in total submission. But, after the passage of years he realized that it was never going to be. When she returned after her confinement, with the baby, he could feel a marked change in her attitude. She was no more her vulnerable self and as days passed, he understood that she was drawing her strength from their little son, who had, by then, occupied her entire world, encroaching even whatever little space was available to his father so long. That was the moment he started hating his son, more than his wife.

It thrilled him on finding that hurting the boy through neglect and deprivation, brought back the same kind of pain and fear back into her eyes, but not for long. She transformed into an aggressive tigress when it came to protecting her young one and this made him a little nervous at times. The more he tried to hurt him, the stronger she grew. She seemed to read his mind and was always prepared with a counter-move or a counter-statement for whatever he did or said and slowly and slowly distanced herself from him, with her son clinging tight to her all the while.

Irritated by her attitude of aloofness, he resorted to disgorge venom at her through his disparaging comments and abusive insinuations. He knew that she was at times really hurt by his crafty, stinging tongue though she veiled it well. She slowly had developed a kind of immunity to the gross apathy that encompassed her existence in that house, which she knew would never be a home to her.

Sometimes she would sit quietly, lost in thoughts, pretending to listen to some weird music of hers and observing her swollen eyes when the music ended would thrill him greatly. Knowing that it was his moment, he would go for it and start his verbal assault.

Once, after upsetting her over a triviality and wanting to have more than his usual quantum of fun, he casually referred to their son as 'that bastard'.

That immediately brought her back to life.

'I wish he is one rather than yours. Both of us, me and him, would then have something to feel more proud about.'

Raju was caught off-guard and had not anticipated this kind of reaction. He hissed, 'You disgusting female, what are you talking?'

Emboldened by his shock she simply said, 'Leave him alone! If you try to hurt him again I will declare to the entire world, especially to your gossiping relatives, that he is a bastard and that is why you hate him. I am past caring about my reputation and will ensure that you get all their sympathies as a cuckold.' Her new-found strength was born out of Raju's obsession for respectability in his society.

Raju started exercising utmost care from then on. He even tried to get closer to the boy in an attempt to create a divide between mother and son and shatter her, one last time; but the boy kept slithering out of his hold all the time. It was once again a stale-mate between father and son. As years went by, each maintained a cordial distance from the other and ensured that their paths seldom crossed.

'No, we can't have any more of that nonsense. Remember you have a sixteen year old son and still, you cannot adjust to people around and blame it on everybody else. You see, we just have fulfilled all our responsibilities and started a peaceful retired life– me and your father– and please don't spoil our peace and happiness with your imaginary problems. Your in-laws are so nice and cordial and Raju is a gem. How can you blame them? You know, how I had suffered at the hands of your grandmother those days. None of you bothered about her caustic remarks and your father was too busy to know what was going on around him. When you go to another house, you need to compromise on certain things and step down from your ivory tower. You know about my background and see how I have put up with life in a small town without complaining. *Appa* was of course so supportive yet…' her mother was going on and on with her usual sermon on the nobility of suffering on the part of married women and how to make a martyr of oneself.

This seemed to be her only way of stopping Ranjani from telling out her woes to her parents. Ranjani knew that her mother was incapable of handling any serious situation, thanks to the protective concern of her father, and was insensitive to such situations in other people's life, even her own daughter's. She had not come out of her *Mills and Boons* age and could never play a supportive role. On the other hand she expected to be pampered at all times and secretly resented the special affection shared between father and daughter. Ranjani looked up at her father sitting opposite to her, looking deep into her eyes and her eyes welled up with unshed tears.

'Don't cry *ma*, sometimes life surprises you with unexpected turns. Come out of your idealism and analyse things practically. What have you got now? A nice family, a respectable job, you keep qualifying yourself more and more and definitely your entire family must be backing you.'

'No *appa*, it is not *because* of them. It is *inspite* of them that I have been achieving more and more, just to escape that dreadful stifling world. They can't tolerate the sight of anything vibrant and alive. If I stay on I will die before times.' She was inconsolable and her father became pensive. He could not bear the sight of his dear girl shedding tears at age forty-two.

As he was about to tell something, the phone rang and he went to the drawing room. He still had not got a mobile phone and said that he would rather be called old fashioned than carry a gadget wherever he went and complicate his life.

The moment he left, her mother started again, 'You are very imaginative and make a mountain out of a mole hill. Why do you make life miserable for us? Have we not done enough and suffered enough for your sake? You are educated and suppose to be very intelligent and you should not be reacting like a simple woman. Your family is away because your husband got transferred to Bangalore. Who told you not to go? What you are doing is not right! You cannot refuse to be with your family because of your job. Anyway, why do you want to work, when your husband is earning well and taking good care of you? You know, he is really very fond of you and must be missing you a lot. Moreover, the boy is more attached to you than anyone else. At least for his sake you should have accompanied them rather than stubbornly clinging to that college of yours.'

Ranjani turned incredulous. So, the skunk had told them that she had refused to go with them, wherein, actually she was left behind deliberately, even though she said she could resign and find a similar job in Bangalore, if necessary. She could not bear to be away from her son and was really concerned about him.

In his chirpy tone he had reassured just the night before they left, 'Don't worry Ranji, I can survive and I'm a big boy. You need a break and be rid of them for a couple of years at least. We can stay in touch, anyway I'll be here for the vacations. I promise, I won't desert camp and join the opposite party. Actually, that is precisely what the fox and the vixen are hoping for. Forget it! It won't happen. Let me also have the taste of life in a big city.'

Now Ranjani could not find a reply to her mother and sat quietly, rather not feeling upto it. Her mother went into the drawing room. In a few seconds, she could be heard telling her father, 'It's nothing. She is a bit depressed and misses her son and husband. She is also overworked, what with her college work and the part-time MBA classes she has started attending! Tell her to spend some time here with us before we leave for Canada.'

Her parents had settled in the same city after her father's retirement and lived in a locality, which was just five minutes drive from her house. She knew why her mother wanted her there. She could do with an efficient hand like Ranjani, who would be able to take care of the house and cooking, while the two old people would be busy with their travel arrangements and shopping.

Her father was too sharp not to read the eagerness in her tone. 'Let her be. She is most welcome to this house. But both of us would become too busy to even spend time with her. Don't force her.'

She was very thankful to her father, so understanding and concerned as always. 'No *ma*, I'll stay in my house. Moreover, I can't leave *Nila* at the mercy of the servant. I won't trouble you, never ever. Enjoy yourself and you can just forget me. See you *pa*. I'll look you up this week end.'

Her father eyed her strangely and simply said, 'Cheer up my girl. Keep your intellect sharp and integrity intact, come what may. You will find peace and happiness.'

Ranjani came out and started her scooter. Like always, her efforts to reach out to her father for some moral support had been thwarted by her loving mom. With all her claims of modernistic outlook and benevolence, her mother was a typical mom of her age, refusing to come out of those social norms, which were meant to ensure the so called security for her kind. Her honour thrived through the act of sweeping anomalies under the carpet, in an effort to maintain respectability, like a hypocrite.

As such, she was not so happy with the household of Ranjani, about which, she could not boast much to her circle of friends. She took pride in the fact that her other two children had settled abroad, enabling her to visit them frequently thereby, making the retired life really meaningful and glorious. Ranjani could feel her mother's resentment clearly, when her siblings visited India. Her mother would start her preparations months ahead and expect Ranjani to take up a bulk of the responsibilities. At times Ranjani would secretly yearn for such care and attention for herself, once in a way, wherein, she could escape the drudgery of her terrible world into the soothing balmy confines of her maternal home like every other woman, but would immediately console herself that she was doomed to be out of the ordinary in everything.

Well, all that Ranjani could now do would be to enjoy her solitude, rejuvenate her sinking spirit and prepare herself. She understood fully the intention of her husband and mother-in-law to leave her behind when he was transferred. It was to demonstrate to her that she was not indispensible and thus shatter her, and at the same time make the world see her as an arrogant, inconsiderate, self-centered, career-oriented woman, who had no familial bonding.

Now, she was in charge of her life on a day-to-day basis and knew that she could either make it or break it. Her marriage had been a disaster and had deprived her of the essential and elemental aspects required for sustenance- recognition, love and acceptance- to be recognised as a fellow being, entitled to her due share in life, to be loved with no demands or expectations and to be accepted as such with her plus and minus, which made up her essence and to be nurtured with real care and concern.

With a new resolve never to take her problems to anyone anymore, including her parents, she became determined to straighten one or two things first. Her actions must, at the same time, not jeopardize her son's chances of ever getting his father's support and concern, especially when he needed them the most. Incidentally, she also knew pretty well that her chances of ever getting on to the main-track was quite remote and that she must choose her moment to call quits.

Blinded by tears of rage, she spewed the words aloud, 'You dirty bastard, you have deprived me of everything that is due to me. You just wait! When you need me the most, when you yearn for the care and love of your family, I'll ensure that you get none. You can gloat over your male ego and eat it up for dinner right now.' With a new resolve, Ranjani revved up her scooter and drove down the lonely road towards her house.

Suddenly she found herself going off-track and driving up the road that led to the temple on the small hillock close to her colony. As usual, she did not go up to the temple. Stopping two hundred meters before, she parked her scooter on the roadside and walked to the rock, twenty meters from the road. It was her favourite spot. She tucked her sari up and climbed the throne and sat on it. Her pulse raced and she felt as if she was getting recharged by the rocky reassurance.

3

I make my song!

The photograph presented an unusual scene and Shree stood in front of it, totally mesmerized by the terrifying ferocity permeating out of the little cat-mom's eyes. She was about to attack a pack of huge dogs. The cat was standing between the dogs and her hapless litter of three kittens, probably just a few days old. Shree was walking around the gallery exhibiting the works of a person whose name was not familiar to her. Mili and Abi were at the costume designer, deciding on the reception dress and Shree, not wanting to project any of her views that might hamper their choice, just excused herself with a headache and walked into the gallery next door that now hosted a photo-exhibition. She found herself drawn to this particular picture and was deeply troubled by the mixture of anguish and ferocity in the eyes of the little mother. She was rather irritated by the apparent callousness of the photographer, who must have been so heartless as to focus on his mission rather than embarking on a rescue operation.

'What a fighter she was! Those dogs were so scared to approach her for some time.'

She turned around and stared straight into the twinkling eyes of a trim looking middle aged man with unkempt salt and pepper crest, clad in a casual T-shirt and a pair of jeans and sporting a pair of shoes with spikes like those used by runners. His French beard looked equally coarse as his hair, which he had tied up in a very short ponytail, and altogether, he looked a bit rugged yet dignified.

'Thaman, the author of these photographs,' he offered an introduction, extending his hand.

'Shree'. After the brief handshake she asked, 'So, the excellent photo was made out of the supreme sacrifice of the cat family, right?' she could not hide the sarcasm in her voice.

He roared with laughter, 'So that was your concern. Thought you were admiring it. I'm not so heartless. After clicking a couple of shots, I had shooed away the dogs and called up Blue Cross and stood guard till the family was rescued.'

'Good to know that', she quipped with an attitude that suddenly seemed to have mellowed. He walked along, offering some kind of explanation or anecdote to each and every photograph and what struck her as odd was that every single one of them evoked some kind of emotion in the onlooker, be it the one portraying humans or sub-humans. The passions were livid and raw on the visage of every creature portrayed and Shree was simply mesmerised.

'Lovely', she murmured as they came to the end of the gallery.

'So, that's all I get- an absent minded remark- for all the trouble I have taken for the shots and for this guided tour in particular', he remarked in a matter of fact manner.

Shree was a little embarrassed and she found it rather unusual. 'No, it's not that. What I mean is, well, I have no words, for I could empathise with all your models, every one of them. Honestly, they are too good.'

Thaman gave a broad grin. 'Well I very rarely get such an understanding and appreciative spectator and that's the reason I took you around so that you don't miss out anything.'

'So you are a professional photographer, right? But I'm sorry, I don't remember seeing your work featured in any magazine, for that matter, I...' suddenly she stopped on realising what she was about to say.

He gave a mischievous smile with his eyes twinkling, 'For that matter, you have not even heard of me.'

Shree felt stupid. How could he talk as if he read her mind? Right from the beginning, she had felt a peculiar feeling of having met him before, but was not quite sure. Though she was certain that this was the first time she had heard an unusual name as his, it was rather confusing.

Again he spoke, 'We must have met before, may be in our previous birth.'

'What? How?' she was really agitated now.

'Cool, cool, it is meant to be a compliment to someone who understood my work. By the way, may I ask what brought you here? You don't appear to be one endowed with such an artistic pursuit as to visit galleries and exhibitions. Was it accidental?'

Shree could not control her giggles now. 'Well, my son, along with his fiancée, is at the designer's next door and I strayed out. No regrets. In fact, I am happy I came here.'

'Hmmmm… you do sound convincing. I owe you one for that. Can I have the honour of having a cup of coffee with you?'

Shree was hesitant and without thinking looked at her watch.

'There is a small cafeteria right outside and your kids can't miss you when they step out of the designer's.' He started walking towards the place and Shree simply joined him. She felt strange at her most uncharacteristic behaviour. Something must have gotten into her.

'So what do you do, other than chaperoning your son and his girl?'

'No it is not what you think. I want to be rid of them, for it looks so odd when I get dragged along with them'.

'Okay, no offence, I can see that you are not gooseberrying. Or else you would not have left them and taken refuge amidst my photographs.' He said in a condescending tone.

Shree was now talking with her customary ease, assuaging his curiosities but ensured that she never transcended beyond professional and academic information about herself.

Thaman read the caution in her demeanor and did not press on. He also gave her bits and pieces of information about him. He had had a successful tenure as the vice-president of an MNC until about a year back and had called it a day to go after his passions-'...photography, travel, adventure, cooking, music ...', he did not complete the list and suddenly looked up at her inquisitively.

'*Ji*... aah, you are here? Thanks for the long wait!' Abi's approaching voice could be heard. He stopped on seeing her companion and Shree made the introductions.

'Congratulations! So, you are going to plunge headlong into family life. You both make a good pair', Thaman eyed the blushing Mili and suddenly said, 'I would like to shoot a few pics of you both sometimes to appease my artistic thirst.'

'Sure uncle', Mili was beyond herself with excitement. Abi got busy chattering with him and after some time they were exchanging business cards, which obviously went well with Abi's gregarious nature. Then Thaman extended one to Shree and got her mobile number, and they promised each other to stay in touch.

They did that precisely, and not a day passed without Thaman talking to either Abi or Shree or sometimes to both of them. Once in a way Thaman and Shree met in some coffee shop when Abi and Mili would be busy otherwise. Shree was able to off-load her fears and trepidations when he was around and he was a patient listener and proved to be a friend in need more than often. She was surprised to find him down to earth and practical, and totally devoid of that halo she invariably found people of his caliber and background donning.

Shree could let go of her reserve and be at ease with him the same way, she did with her son or brother. Yet, at times she felt that there was something familiar, though mysterious at the same time, with his ways, especially the way he interacted with her and she could not put her finger exactly into it.

'Good job. Only a super woman like you could have done it alone', Thaman put a patronising arm round her shoulder and said in a voice that betrayed real emotions.

'I was not alone. The two kids were with me all the time and a great friend offered his shoulders to rest whenever I wilted under pressure', she said and patted his hands affectionately.

The wedding reception had just gotten over and Abi was busy supervising the winding up.

Thaman was all along very busy with his camera and had been capturing all kinds of emotions that pervaded throughout the evening. He now pulled a chair and started checking on those shots one by one and suddenly, stopped and looked up at her. By now she had also slumped on a chair nearby, exhausted. She gently pulled the monitor to her side and was surprised to see her picture. She was scrutinising a piece of paper, totally oblivious of her surrounding that was buzzing with varied activities.

'You always do that, don't you?'

'What?' she could not comprehend.

'Go into the heart of things and lose yourself.' As if he could not bear to see her confusion he suddenly got up and said, 'Shree, it's time to catch up with your sleep. Tomorrow you have to go to the court for the first hearing. You need to stay fresh. I'll drive you down, if you don't mind.'

'Oh no, I am going alone. Advocate Mithra is in town. In fact, he was here this evening and has assured me all guidance and assistance. Moreover, it is my battle, my burden. I don't want to make it a joint venture and that's why I told Abi and Mili to keep out of it. Thanks, I don't need a cross-bearer.'

A crooked smile brightened his face. 'Aha, I see it now, my dear strong woman. You are afraid that our concern and care would weaken you. Okay have it your way. All the best!' Once again he shook her hand and walked out, vanishing into the night.

Shree suddenly felt alone for a few minutes but once again started deriving her strength from her solitude. The strong feeling that she had none to lean on and there was no one to cherish and take care of her had made her self-reliant and strong. Her few friends had marvelled at her ability to stay calm during crisis, all along.

Sujatha, who was pretty close to her these past years, once said to her, 'Shree, there is some kind of stillness about you, especially when everything around you is in a turmoil. You strike me odd as the eye of the cyclone, which practically is a vacuum.'

Shree laughed and simply asked, 'Hey Suji! Are you implying that I am empty and devoid of substance?'

It was the finale of a funny conversation that they had just five hours after a terrible accident Shree had met with, which could have easily finished her off.

Shree had given her car for service and rode her scooter that particular day. She had in fact waited for her son to leave for Goa with a couple of friends, since he was using the scooter then. The traffic was less on that second Saturday and as she approached the signal at the intersection just before her destination, she slowed down as the signal turned amber, preparing to stop. Right then, a van overtook her on the left and probably, the driver, in a hurry to shoot beyond before the signal

144

turned red, accelerated and simultaneously moved to his right to avoid hitting another vehicle on his left, trapping Shree's huge *Activa* between his van and the median.

The longest agonizing fifteen seconds finally threw Shree off her vehicle, onto the road on the opposite side, after the vehicle she rode got dragged till the end of the median, just a few meters before the signal post. Luckily, since the signal had turned red by then, the opposite side of the road she rolled on was free, excepting a few pedestrians who were crossing.

Shree never had imagined that one would be able to do so much of musing in just fifteen seconds!

'Oh God, I'm done!' was the very first of her thoughts.

Then she screamed at the driver of the van who was just adjacent to her vehicle, 'Idiot, stop!' at which, he panicked and accelerated further.

'So, what is it going to be like?' she prepared herself for her end.

Suddenly she remembered that she was not wearing her helmet and as she started tilting towards the road, she pulled her head away towards left and received the full impact of the fall on her right shoulder, all the while uttering a silent prayer, 'Ma *Kali*, please make it quick and painless'.

Well, it was painless initially as she rolled and sat up in the middle of the road. She was a bit disoriented but realized that she was breathing and alive, yet all the while fighting a blackout. She could see blood all over her legs and dress and some on the road too.

People crossing the road ran to her and when someone tried to lift her, she hissed with all ferocity, 'Don't touch me! Let me first check what is broken.' The ring of bystanders went aghast and moved out a little. Shree slowly got up staggered a bit, ambled to the pavement and sat on it planting her feet on the road. By then someone had extracted her handbag from the mangled scooter and tried to open it in a bid to find her cell-phone. Shree simply extended her left hand, got the bag, placed it on her lap, opened it and extracted the device. Next, she dialled her colleague Sujatha's number, hoping she had already reached their place which was just half a kilometer away.

Sujatha had actually taken the day off to attend the parents' meet in her son's school. Anyway, she immediately alerted the others and within minutes, three of her colleagues reached the spot but stood rooted near her on seeing the blood on her clothes and the condition of her vehicle.

'Hey, guys what's wrong with you? One of you please take care of my vehicle. Gentlemen, could you kindly escort a damsel in distress to the hospital? I might be in terrible pain, mind you!'

They then started reacting fast, with Shree giving some instruction or reminder once in a way. It was not so easy to stay alert, conscious and up anymore, still she was managing.

At last, when she was wheeled through the hospital corridor, gritting her teeth, she just smiled and said, 'Thanks guys! Now get back to work! Sujatha will be here any minute. The junior most of her friends said, 'A boss is always a boss, madam. And you really terrify me.'

A couple of minutes later, when the doctor touched her right leg near the ankle, she screamed in pain and fainted- at last!

Sujatha had rushed to the hospital with her husband Ram and both of them took care of the situation and Shree. Ram called up Shree's husband, who arrived two hours later, complaining all the way about Shree's rashness and literally shouting at a feeble Shree with bandaged arms and legs, for causing a lot of inconvenience to him- the busiest professional in the city- who had lots of clients queued up at his office for their scheduled appointments. His vanity had infuriated Sujatha, and as she was about to open her mouth in quick reproach Ram's calm voice silenced her.

'Sir, don't worry. We will take care of madam. There is a minor crack in her wrist, which is now plastered and a bad concussion on her shoulder. It is actually the aberrations all along her right leg that cause all the pain and discomfort, though the surgeon has cleaned and bandaged it all.'

His patient update of the situation had irritated the two ladies. Sujatha was just flabbergasted that the insensitive moron had not only taken his own sweet time to visit his injured wife but also had not bothered to find out how she was doing. On the other hand, he was complaining, implying that her unfortunate accident had impeded the proceeding of his day. So ridiculous!

After Ram assured him that he and Sujatha would drop Shree at home in the evening and he wouldn't need to break up any meeting and come back, he left brusquely without even a word of thanks. Ram moved away silently shaking his head in utter disbelief and it was then that Sujatha called Shree the eye of the storm.

That night, in her bed, wreathing in agony, (her wonderful husband had managed to discard those painkillers from her pouch of medicines) Shree realised that she had the ability to grow insensitive to physical pain if she could focus on other immediate things at hand, like it happened at the time of her accident that morning.

Well, she almost had a date with death but not quite, and thinking of it made her more frivolous than serious. For the first time the absurdity that she believed to be life made itself tangible and hit her on the face. What if she had died? Would that be the end of her life, her everything, the end of *her*? So, had she been frantic to stay alive so as to just carry on with her struggle?

Suddenly, she realised that it was not worth at all.

Why must she glorify her existence as life, when she had literally missed the most essential element that defined life?

If she had died that morning that would be the end of her life and her battle, but what exactly was she fighting and what for?

So, all along her life had been nothing but the fight. Once it was won or lost, what else would be there in it to look forward to?

The more she thought, the clearer she understood her predicament.

For the first, time she could see what it meant to be alive or to really feel alive and her passion for life multiplied exponentially.

'*Ji*, I don't like your latest move. What is the need for you to move out? True, your mom is back after her long stay abroad, but she is self-sufficient at age 75 and does not need you to look after her. Why are you doing this to us, especially when Urmila is in her early stages of pregnancy?'

Shree looked at her fuming son and gave her usual cool, complacent smile. 'Well, you do take good care of your wife, and moreover, I am not going out of town. I'll be moving just fifteen kilometers away, thirty minutes drive at the most. Moreover that place is closer to my office.'

Of late, she got a hunch that the two youngsters had started looking up to her for everything, including a decision on the day's menu. Initially, Shree did not mind it and allowed them their share of conjugal bliss that would veil all mundane interests and take them on their rosy path. Yet she felt that it was time to make them get grounded to reality and take stock of what life held for just the two of them and decided to remove the protective shield that her mere presence had been offering, rendering a cushioning effect. It so coincided with her mother's return from the US and she decided to move in with her, much to the displeasure of Mili.

When she first declared her decision to Thaman the previous week, while sipping their casual coffee at the usual coffee shop, he just smiled and said, 'I know, you can never play the role of a mother-in-law ever. Well,

Shree, you are not a lady at all, I mean not the regular kind, and I respect you for that.'

'Jokes apart, do you think I can do it without any guilt feeing? Am I forsaking the kids?'

'Why do you ask me?' he looked into her eyes.

On receiving no response, he continued, 'Understand one thing, my dear. True love is never demanding. It is to let go or else it becomes stifling. Love should not smother and in turn get snuffed out.'

Shree could not resist a chuckle. 'A confirmed bachelor, talking of true love!'

'A small correction Madam. I never ever bragged that I am a confirmed bachelor. I have had my own share of girlfriends and relationships and you know about most of those. Probably you can say that I never received the right quantum of true love.'

'Well that makes the two of us,' she remarked casually.

'No Shree. We are different. Tell me honestly, have you ever given all your love to someone... someone special? Well, I am not talking about your son or your family... hope you understand... the one with whom you would have wanted to bond and share everything throughout life?' He paused, looked deep into her perplexed eyes and continued, 'Someone who should have been the substance of your sustenance and the essence of your existence'

'Wow! I like that! With all these alliterations, Thams, I never could imagine you to be so romantic', she broke into peels of laughter and for the first time, her laughter irritated Thaman.

'Be a bit serious and behave your age *Ji...* ' He barked at her and suddenly stopped short.

Shree looked up, shocked by his rage and held back another funny quip.

His eyes softened suddenly. *'Ji...* Shree, be honest with yourself. At any point of time, have you ever felt that your life would be incomplete without a special someone? He paused a little, 'Well... I have.'

Shree just froze, her face went blank and she sat motionless like a statue.

'Sorry, I don't mean to intrude into your privacy. Forget it.'

'It's okay. What you say is true. I have never felt it all these years.'

'And why, may I ask?'

She looked a little confused. 'Probably, because I never received any love, the kind that I could have reciprocated.'

'Shree, don't continue to fool yourself. With your looks, intelligence and, may be, I'll put it this way, for being the person you are, you must have had a million admirers, men who would have given you anything, their entire life, all the love... just to have you around.'

'Ha ha... you *are* a romantic Thaman. Things just don't happen that way in real life.'

'The problem with you is, you don't look beyond yourself. What if there had been someone who had felt madly for you but had not expressed it for fear of being rejected?'

Shree could not fully grasp what he was trying to tell.

Thaman gently continued. 'Men make a lot of blunders when it comes to expressing real feelings.'

Shree looked up sharply, 'Have you?'

'What?

'Committed such blunder?'

Suddenly Thaman became very pensive. 'It was not a blunder. It was deliberate. I did not express my mind but decided to let go.'

She was shocked. 'Why would you do that and ruin your life?'

Thaman became once again his composed self. 'I told you, true love is to let go. She was so precious, so full of life and spirit and I did not have it in me to confine her in my heart and suffocate her with my love. I had always been fascinated by her nascent feral impulses that marked her uniqueness. So I thought I would wait for her to come back to me.'

'Where is she now? When did you let go of her?'

'Oh, that was about three decades back.'

She was incredulous. 'What are you talking, my friend? Don't tell me that you are still waiting for her!'

'Aha, yes. I can sense that she is on her way back to me. Must have gone one full circle by now.' He suddenly turned his own mischievous self once again, threw back his head and laughed, the old twinkle returning to his eyes.

Shree was in no mood for any joke or laughter and sat quietly.

'So, when are you moving. I see that you have packed all your things. Tell me in advance so that I can get a suitable cargo carrier.' Shree heard Abi talking from a distance and came out of her reverie.

'Aah, yes… what did you say?'

'There you go again! How can you keep zooming in and out? At this rate, one of these days you are going to land aplomb into your previous birth or next birth.'

Shree was happy that Abi was once again his usual self. He was quite pragmatic and never mixed emotions with planning- just like her. But with Mili things were different. At times she was bewildered by their ways but understood them to be the best. Her love for her husband and admiration for her mother-in-law were so strong that she would follow them blindly with complete trust. Shree would caution her against this kind of faith and tell her to exercise her option whenever there was a choice. Yet Mili would simply say, 'No ma, you both know the best and I feel very safe and I will go any length with you both.'

Shree outlined her plan and expressed her desire to shift to her mom's place at the earliest. She realised that she was getting averse to the very thought of staying in one place for long and probably that was the reason why she had taken up a new job that called for a bit of travelling once in a way.

'Fine, I'll do the needful. But don't forget that your rightful place is with us- me, Mili and our kids.'

'Kids? How many are coming?' she resumed her normal attitude with him.

'Oh, not sure, may be at least half a dozen', replied Abi with a twinkle in his eyes.

'My best wishes to all of you.' Now she could not control herself and burst out laughing.

PART IV

EPIPHANY

1

Entrapped

Life was getting rather complicated and Gina found herself at the crossroads wondering which way to take. She was rather irritated to see everyone around looking at her rather as an object to be disposed away by getting her married off. She had been teaching English in her own school at the request of the Head-mistress, right from the very next day she wrote the last paper of her PG examination. Even before she could think of her every next plan, people had been making decisions on her behalf and she was rather disgruntled. Her aspirations for research were put down firmly by her mother, who would rather see her married off happily. 'Happily, for whom?' She once asked to everybody's displeasure. Why do people assume that she was also in a hurry to get married to find the ultimate bliss?

'*Amma*, please leave me alone for some time. I don't say that I will not get married but right now I am not ready', she once implored when her mother started talking about some prospective groom suggested by her relative.

'Gina, don't be ridiculous! You are already twenty-three and well accomplished. What more do you want?' retaliated her mother. If you want you can enroll for any number of courses even after marriage and pursue your studies. Already you are doing your second post-graduation in Psychology. Don't link up extraneous things with married life.'

'It is not that *ma*. How can I take a total stranger to be my everything, just because I get married to him?' Gina ran out of words and did not know how to make her mother understand her. The effort was one of trying to wake a person, who was pretending to be asleep, up. She could understand the concern of her mother, who had of late been facing a lot of queries from far-away friends, nosy neighbours and relentless relatives about Gina's future plans, especially her marriage. Some were even pointing their fingers at her parents for giving too much of freedom to a girl.

Some of Gina's friends who were married and had one or two children and looking huge like hippopotamuses very often caught her mother's attention, of late. She also probably wanted to go around boasting about her married daughter's impending visits and confinements, taking pride in the new prospective role of a mother-in-law or grandmother.

Gina kept such conversations at bay by deliberately staying aloof. She suddenly felt terribly alone, with not a single soul to share her mind. She had a lot of questions. Why do people assume her to be like every one of her friends? Can she not make any decision regarding her life? What is wrong with her? Why can't she ever agree with any of those *normal* things? She started to feel wretched and miserable and totally misfit and horribly insufficient. Her sense of self-worth took a dip to the worst possible low and as usual on comparing herself with her friends and siblings she felt grossly inadequate.

She thought and thought, and failing to get any clarity, decided to dump those horrible thoughts and continued with her work at school. In fact, she enjoyed every minute of it and could easily connect with her pupils. Her ability to not only teach English but also get her students ready for cultural programmes with a skit or musical performance was really amazing. Her own teachers, including Suganthi madam, who now were her colleagues, never missed an opportunity to boast to the rest of the school as to what they could do to a willing and avid learner, pointing at the versatile Gina.

Gina could not understand why *Amma* was too eager to spend more time with her of late. She would call her out for a walk in the evening and pick up a conversation during the casual stroll. Any topic she started would slowly progress into the inevitable theme of marriage and Gina was getting exasperated. It was getting worse day by day and at last one day, Gina burst out, 'Why are you so bent upon getting rid of me?'

Her mother was taken aback by the ferocity in her voice, but recoiled immediately, 'Don't be naïve Gina, you are trying to run away from life. Whether you want it or not, we need to fulfil our obligation to our daughter and you have no say in this. We are not trying to chase you out of the house as you think. See all your friends and classmates, all are married and have one or two kids and some, even three. Of course we didn't try to rush things as soon as you finished school like in most of their cases, but remember, you are almost twenty four and your sister is completing her studies this year and will be ready in a couple of years. We need to plan everything as your father is also due for his retirement next year. Please understand. Why are you not normal ever?'

Gina was stunned and for the first time felt like an intruder in her own house, little realizing that this feeling was there to stay forever. Her mother was more concerned about the ire and criticism of friends and family rather than Gina's real fears and trepidations. All that could have settled Gina's nerves was a little bit of maternal reassurance, but all that she got was criticism that instilled doubts and made her lose all sense of self worth.

Once again Gina got the feeling that she had grown into a great nonconformist and a misfit, which had landed her parents in a precarious predicament. Whose fault was that? All along, she had heard of her mother boasting about her eldest daughter's unusual traits that set her apart from girls her age, but now everything was viewed differently when it came to matters concerning matrimony. She made no ado about hiding her displeasure over Gina's self acquired intelligence that was making her a sceptic, her tastes, preferences and other such odd things, which according to her, would mar a normal married life. Moreover, what mattered more to her mother was her own security, which would be the resultant of fulfilling all her responsibilities and settling down in a carefree retired life with her husband, like most other ladies her age.

Gina wanted to scream and bang her head on something but simply said, 'Okay, do as you wish,' and abruptly entered the house and started walking towards the staircase leading to the open terrace. As she set her foot on the first of the flight of steps, she turned her head and called out to her mother, 'The earlier you send me out the better…for you.'

'Do you like the design Gina?' her mother's voice was brimming with affection, which Gina had never experienced so far.

'Does it matter, now that you have already finalised it?'

'Don't be a spoilsport Gina. Everyone is so excited and you, the bride, should be the happiest. *Appa* has taken all the pains and found a good match for you. At this young age your fiancé is already the manager in a bank and the family is a nice one. May be he is a little dark in complexion compared to you but is still tall and handsome and has really taken a liking for you. What more can a girl ask for? I don't *understand* your sulking! You don't want to come for any shopping and you have asked *appa* to select everything including the invitation card. Cheer up Gina! I'll tell you something; this period of engagement is the most memorable phase in one's life. Better start corresponding with him so that you get to know each other.'

Gina just listened to her mother with her characteristic absent-mindedness, little realising then, that later she would regret for not paying heed to the last part of her sermon.

'Gina, are you kidding?' her sister, Jayji looked at her with utter disbelief. She had just written her final semester examination and had immediately packed up and vacated her hostel, to spend at least a few happy days with Gina, before the latter's marriage. She expected Gina to be in cloud nine and wanted to hear about the prospective brother-in-law. But, all that she could find was Gina in her usual corner in their library, reading *Atlas Shrugged* contrary to her expectation that she would, at least now, be reading some romance.

Further, when she learnt that she was not corresponding with her would-be-husband, nor had they even contacted each other over phone, she could not believe it.

'Hey, what is there to talk now? After all we will be having a whole life time to do that', Gina tried to sound light but her voice quivered.

Of late, the sisters had become very close, that is, ever since the younger one went to the hostel. They were totally different on many counts, yet bonded very well. They both had realised how much they missed each other.

'Okay, tell me. At least, when he came to see you with his parents, did you both talk?'

'Of course, *Appa* told me show him our library, but he was actually not interested in seeing the books but rather went on talking about his job, mother, family, and such mundane things.'

'That's all? He didn't ask anything about you?'

'Oh yes, he wanted to know if any boy had proposed to me, saying it is quite understandable in the case of good looking girls.'

'What? He really asked that? What did you say?

Gina threw back her head and laughed. 'I asked him whether he had the habit of proposing to every good-looking girl he came across. Obviously, he didn't like it and changed the topic back to how his mother had sacrificed everything to raise her three children.'

'By the way, what's his full name? I keep hearing only the first part of it all the time.'

'Oh, some Mohan', Gina replied nonchalantly.

'*Some* Mohan?'

'Does it matter? He made it clear that his mother may not like me calling him by name and she is averse to short names and pet names. So I am also going to become nameless- *Anamika.*' She again gave a wry chuckle.

'Gina, Gina... what made you say 'yes' to this person?'

'Any way, I have to say that to someone, someday, right? So I did it in the very first instance.'

'Then?'

'Jayji, don't look so upset. I am happy, can't you see that?'

'Gina...' suddenly her sister hugged her and started weeping. In between sobs she continued, 'I want to say that I am happy for you but I am not able to do it.'

Gina's eyes brimmed with tears and she affectionately held on to her sister.

The last of the marriage rituals got over and Gina was being packed off to her new home. Gina came to where her father was sitting. He was totally exhausted but quite happy for his favourite child. Her mother-in-law was all smiles and told him, 'She becomes my girl from today. We will take good care of her. You need not have any anxiety over her.' Gina found herself crying inconsolably, when she found her father a bundle of emotions for the first time.

The long car ride was rather tiring and by the time she reached her new home, in the new city, with her new family, she was completely worn out. She suddenly remembered her mother's caution just before leaving.

'Don't just walk in as soon as you reach your home. They will do a *Haarthi,* and you will be taken in with some ceremony. So be a little gentle and lady-like.'

She hesitated at the doorstep and the entire family simply walked in.

'What are you waiting for? Do you need a special invitation? This is *our* house and *you* are going to be here henceforth.' She was perplexed by the tone and attitude of her mother-in-law that had drastically changed to one of dominance and acrimony and she simply stood rooted there. Blinking away her tears, she just looked at her husband, who was standing behind his mother.

He said, 'Come in, I will show you our room, so that you can get settled.' She followed him like a lamb and when she saw the new bed selected and sent by her father, along with the other pieces of furniture there, she realised how tired she was and how much she wanted to sleep.

He simply continued, 'I have to go out. Will be back in an hour. Have your dinner with the others. *Don't wait for me.'*

Gina felt herself rudely shaken out of her deep sleep. She was totally disoriented.

Where was she?

What was the time?

Who was that shaking her and pulling at her dress?

What was that disgusting smell?

She sat up on the new bed with a start. She caught a glimpse of her husband in the diffused light from the bathroom.

'Great! How can you fall asleep on our wedding night? He was a bit too loud and she could not understand why his speech was slurred. Before she could reply or move he came very close and bent close to her face. His breath reeked of something she had known in her school chemistry lab. She tried to push him away in utter disbelief and disgust but was overpowered by his vice-like grip. What followed next was the night-marish experience, which would recur and recur in the years to come.

Life had trapped her in a loveless predicament from which there seemed to be no escape!

2

Evolved

'So, you have made the decision and even fixed the date. Wonderful!' Raju was sneering at her, while his mother had pulled a dining chair and was watching the drama with so much of enjoyment, reclining on it.

Ranjani shot back, 'You did not bother to come with me to the doctor and I had no one with me when I underwent all the tests and scans. It's all about me! When she said that I have to undergo the surgery immediately, I had to take a call and fix the time and date. My mother will be assisting me during my stay in the hospital and taking me to their home for rest and recoupment straight from there. Finally, I am going to foot all expenses. So I don't see where you people come in.'

She was surprised at the rancour that showed in her voice. She simply added, 'By the way, I have tabled my papers yesterday. The chairman of my institute is quite reluctant to relieve me, yet when I made it on health reasons and said I would not be able to put up with all the stress, he has agreed on condition that I still remain a member of the college advisory board and render my service as a consultant. So after three months rest, I will come back here to *this* house, my rightful place.'

Ranjani, at age fifty was the Dean in a famous business school in the city, and in fact, one of the most qualified and eligible heads in the University. She had been indiscriminately adding up to her qualifications and just about a month back presented herself for the viva-voce of her second Ph.D degree, this time in Marketing Management.

Her work and studies had filled up the lacuna that was glaring at her right from day one of her association with Raju's family. She had risen to the present position even five years back. Proximity to her college had been the reason quoted by Raju to make her shift to a rented house, twenty kilometers away, to cover up his ulterior motives.

For once Ranjani felt grateful to him and started managing her house, her finances and her life. Once in a way, Raju would come to spend the weekend at her place to try to evoke in her, the memories of her unpleasant times with him as his wife. But added to it, he had one more hidden agenda of making her neighbours believe that he was a doting husband and more so, a conscientious son performing the duties that his wife had failed, to his parents, because of her preference to a career over family.

But, what she alone was aware was that, he spent most of his weekends elsewhere, all the time making his parents and her parents believe that he was at her place.

With their son, it was all together a different story. Matters had soured between father and son to such an extent that they avoided each other deliberately. She could sense that Raju was actually scared of his son but could not figure out anything else. Ultimately, the boy had moved out, not being able to put up with the caustic remarks of the other family members, thanks to the courtesy of his father, who painted a dark picture of him, projecting him as a, dark-horse and more as a worthless loafer, so as to win the sympathy of everyone around and justify his dipsomania, which had by then become an open secret.

He could easily make people remark, 'This is what becomes of a virtuous man who has got for himself an arrogant wife and a prodigal son.'

After his post graduation in Commerce, Nandhu got himself a part time job and was also gearing himself up to become a Charted Accountant. Ranjani had extended him all support, emotional, moral and even financial, but he had gently declined the last one.

When he returned after his two years stint in Bangalore, with the rest of the family, Ranjani noticed the enigmatic change in him. She had sent away a mere boy and he returned a mature man. His sense of independence and rebellion that marked him as a maverick, had instantly terrified her initially, but when she realised that he reflected all her hidden traits quite blatantly, she was very happy for him and rather felt proud of him. He would break all norms, not to get his father's attention but to defy all standards set forth in the household and provoke his father with a fond hope that the latter would disown him.

He moved in with Ranjani, but then, Raju made it a point to visit them more often as if to check on them or rather spoil all the tranquillity that prevailed in their life and upset their plans for the weekends. That was when the young man declared his decision to move out.

Once, in his cool way, he reasoned with his mother over dinner at a quiet joint he had discovered close to the airport.

'Ranji, it is so simple. Technically I will be living in my bachelor's abode, but practically, we will continue the same way as now, so that you can see less of that demon and focus on your research on the one hand and the college administration on the other. This is just a ploy to throw the bugger out. Now a days, I can see the tension writ on your face and you tend to be moody and low more than often. I don't want him to add to your woes. Are you really alright? Did you go for your master health check up? When did you last see your gynic?

'I'm actually fine. Just the usual age related problems for which I am under medication. When are you moving out and where, if I may ask?'

He detailed his plans and she was convinced then.

That was about a couple of years back!

'I'll have none of it! You can go ahead with the surgery as per schedule, but I am bringing you back here. You can have all the rest here. The three of us will take good care of you. You are not going to your parents' house now.'

This was an emphatic declaration from Raju and she was appalled when she realised that the third person he mentioned was their cook, who had found a permanent residence in their home. Worse still, she occupied Nandhu's room, which obviously was one of the reasons for Raju to get his wife out of the house and manage to keep her at bay for the past six years.

Ranjani felt that there is no point in arguing with him, as he would anyway convince her parents that she would get the best attention from his family. Moreover, her father had not been keeping good health of late and was undergoing a series of medical procedures.

Ranjani too had been under medication for the past couple of years and her gynaecologist had ultimately declared that she must undergo a hysterectomy as her fibroids had grown enormously, so enormous that a simpler procedure was totally ruled out. Ranjani had just returned after fixing up the date with Dr. Geethanjali, and that had generated so much of heat and no concern.

Slowly she moved into her room. She must get busy from the next day, vacating her rented premises and moving her things back. On the way back from the clinic, she dropped in at her parents' and her father immediately conceded to her request to move all her worldly possessions into his house. The big room upstairs was literally empty and he had time and again indicated that either she or her son or both could move into the house anytime. He had started smelling a rat but she would not tell anything now even when asked. Her mother as usual was in her happy world, far removed from reality.

She could hear her mother-in-law, 'What are we going to do with the useless woman after her surgery? She won't be of any use to me or you or to *our* house. Moreover, she has decided not to work anymore and she is going to become a liability, a burden. Let her go to her parents' house and not return.'

'Shhh... *Amma* you are tactless. She must be made to go on her own. Please, keep quiet. I'll take care of everything.'

Ranjani could hear her tummy grumble and she felt the terrible pangs of hunger eating her up. That was the fifth day after her surgery and she had been discharged from the hospital. Raju acted true to the role he was playing and brought her back, deposited her in her room and left for the office, or that's where he said he was going, immediately. He had, by now, soon after his short stay in Bangalore, taken a golden handshake from his bank and started his stint as a private professional. On the way, he dropped his mother-in-law back in her house, thanking her profusely for taking good care of his wife for the past five days, when Ranjani was in the hospital and the old lady was overwhelmed as usual.

Ranjani moved to the kitchen slowly, found an unopened packet of oats and made herself some porridge. The cook as usual had not bothered to consider her for the preparation of meals. As she mouthed her last spoonful, sitting on the bed in her room, she heard the familiar rumble of the *Bullet* and in a minute, her son was standing in front of her. He had been with her in the hospital most of the time and would slip away during visiting hours to avoid Raju.

He started emptying his backpack. First, he took out the entire set of Asimov's *Foundation* Series. Then he brought out a red coloured bound book- *Soundharyalahari!* She remembered telling him that she wanted to memorise all the hundred *Slokas,* and also revive her little knowledge of *Sanskrit*. Then he took out a pile of CDs and DVDs of music and movies of all genres that she would enjoy.

Lastly, he started doing a very odd thing. He hid small packets in different places in the room- some in her wardrobe, some in the dressing table drawer, one behind the TV and he even kept one in the laundry basket.

'Hey, what are those?'

'Home made chocolates, dry fruits, nuts and other yummy things. Truly, I don't expect these morons to feed you. They must be planning to starve you to death and blame it on your poor health. I am keeping a can of fresh juice between the bed and the wall on your side, out of sight for everyone else. Any way keep pretending that you are starving and don't give room for any suspicion! By the way, I have asked the corner shop *anna* to deliver two tender coconuts to you- only to you- one in the morning and one in the evening.

Remember, the doctor said that you need to take a lot of fresh juice and tender coconut milk for at least two weeks.' Finally, he ran out of breath and stopped.

She looked at him speechless. Unshed tears pricked her eyelids. He gently put his strong arms round her. 'Don't you worry, big girl! If you need something, just let me know. I'll look you up day after tomorrow. You see, tomorrow is Sunday and I don't want to bump into that fellow.' With these words he was gone and she heard his vehicle roaring into life again.

He kept his promise and took caution not to leave her out of his sight for longer than twenty-four hours.

It was almost a month and she was having the greatest vacation of her life, much to the amazement of her family. Her son played a vital role in boosting her morale and kept her well nourished. On his way to see her, he would stop at her parents' to collect the soup or pudding her father would have prepared exclusively for her.

It was dusk and she heard his vehicle as usual. She was surprised to hear him honk a couple of times. Someone must have latched up the gate, which he would otherwise push open with his foot and drive through inside and park the vehicle in the portico! People at home had slackened the strict practice of locking up the gate after Nila's passing away a couple of years before.

Ranjani rushed out to open the gate. Exactly at the same moment she emerged out, he too swung his right leg back, in a bid to park the vehicle outside the gate. He felt the gripping pangs of a cramp almost paralysing him in its intense pain and he lost his balance and slid with the vehicle on the left with his leg caught between the frame and the ground, which was a little muddy due to the previous night's rain. He was pinned to the ground and could not move.

She ran out opening the gate. In the meanwhile, two youngsters passing that way rushed to his aid and tried to lift the machine weighing almost 250 kilograms but it would not budge an inch. She bent down, gripped the handle with both her hands and just straightened the *Bullet Machismo*! He slowly got up limped a bit and turned to her and his looks changed more to one of disbelief than shock.

'Ranji… what are you doing? Are you mad?' he yelled at her.

It was only then that she got out of her frenzy and felt the bike weighing heavily in her hands and she felt a sharp, tearing pain in her lower abdomen and started swaying, almost letting go of it. His reflexes were sharp and he caught hold of the machine and kicked the side-stand into position. The two young men, who had initially tried to help, were watching the entire drama in total confusion and bewilderment, just once in a way, calling out to her, 'Madam...Madam...'

She was dazed and walked in like a zombie supported by her son. Before he could open his mouth again, she asked in a whisper, 'What did I do? How did I do it?'

Again, she almost screamed, 'How did I do it *da?*'

He put his arm round her shoulder and gently guided her into her room, towards her bed. She sat silently and drank the water from the bottle he extended to her. She grew calm and her panting subsided.

He started talking gently in his sonorous voice, which was very much like her father's.

'You see Ranji, it is all there. You have it in you, the raw strength. Why don't you see it? You have gone too deep inside yourself to remember what you really are. Why don't you let *her* out? Do you need some disaster to get proactive? One thing I can tell you, you are not safe here anymore and I am terribly worried. You have been pushed too close to the edge and I am scared that you would go over soon, at this rate. Wake up to reality and try to salvage whatever is left of you and your life.'

She neither moved, nor even flickered her eyes. Wearing a glazed look, she dissolved into herself.

There was an absolute stillness about her. Her mind was roaming in all directions and her external demeanour defied the conflict that raged within.

The young man continued, 'It is not just your life I am talking about. I am more worried about my life too. I am bound to this place and this bloody family because you still continue to think of yourself as part of it and I have to consider myself as part of you. I am pleading for my liberation. True, I have moved out, but you make me keep coming back here again and again, in every sense. Can't you see what I am going through? I want to settle down and live my life, but I can't balance on two horses when I finally come to it.' Ranjani was shocked to see his tears.

He continued, 'Know what, I have changed my initials and this has been notified in the gazette too. I don't want any part of that man, not even his name, to go before or after me. I now don't have an initial but just a family name, Bharathwaj, the name of the *Gothra*. I hate everything about here. At this rate, I'll soon start hating you too, if you stay on.'

'What am I to do?' her voice was a mere whisper.

'Don't ask me! Can't you see that you are not part of this family? You never were! Who are you here? Why are you here? Ask yourself.' He abruptly turned and left the room. In a minute, she could hear the rumble of his machine.

It took some time for Ranjani to come out of her stupor. More than the burden of the machine, she felt that his words had weighed her down heavily. Slowly she came out of herself. Poor boy, he had gone through his share of miseries through sheer deprivation and she had been aggravating things by staying quite, all the while living in a delusion. She was on the brink as he implied but hardly had she realized that he too was getting dragged along. He needed to be saved and liberated as much as she.

She again started going inward. Her door was open but she was still at the threshold refusing to pass through. What if she stepped into a void? Anyway, that could not hurt her as there was nothing else on which she would get bashed and shattered in a void, with nothing to break her fall. May be she could float, fly…fly away...

She suddenly became aware of the pain in her abdomen as the weight in her mind started lifting. Yes, as he said it was all there, her liberation and life, intact and unlived and like a fool she had refused to pay heed to its beckon. What should she do now? She had failed to be proactive and help them both out at the initial stages itself, but now she could at least be a little reactive and responsive. She had not gone into a denial mode at all and she had acknowledged her problem and predicament long back. But since then she was sitting on them comfortably and still did not want to move out of her comfort zone.

Funny, a person who was so passionate about everything she did, had failed to carry over the same passion to life! For once, the more she thought, the clearer it became. There is no point in getting involved in those endless battles and euphemize that as life. She found herself fully out of her dazed stupor at last.

Enough is enough!

Ranjani's husband noticed the change in her deportment and he was puzzled by the silence that his caustic remarks evoked instead of the usual sharp sarcastic quips. He was eagerly waiting for an implosion- expecting her to go inward and destroy herself, not being able to withstand the tremendous pressure that he was apparently creating.

Ranjani was sitting on the sofa in the drawing room with the *Soundharyalahari* on her lap. She was trying to focus on the thirty first verse, but her mind was getting frantic.

What a fool she had been! She had failed to live her life but had rather spent it battling the choices thrust on her.

What had she been waiting for?

Was she so foolish as to expect a cave to open up into a tunnel?

Why had she been so reckless and hurt herself?

Was it to prove that she was alive and vibrant?

To whom? Did anybody care?

Can avoidance ever become a solution?

Raju was sitting opposite and watching her face intently. He knew that she was troubled, probably for not being able to see her parents so often as usual, he thought.

Suddenly Raju started a casual conversation with his mother, who was having a hearty meal at the dining table.

'*Ma* they say women go into depression after such a surgery. Is it true?'

The older woman took the hint and immediately replied, 'Of course. There is hormonal imbalance and sometimes they even get suicidal.'

What rubbish! Ranjani started listening to the conversation and realised that it was well rehearsed.

Suddenly Raju got up and stood facing her.

'Ranjani, do you have any such idea?'

She looked up in confusion, 'What do you mean?'

He said in a coaxing tone, 'Obviously, you are depressed. You are not okay and there is something diabolically wrong with you. It is quite a natural aftermath of this surgery. Do you feel like putting an end to this miserable life of yours?' He paused, 'If so please be frank and we can help you out', he had a sheepish grin writ all over his face.

She snapped out of her trance and all her senses got activated suddenly.

Slowly she got up, the book slipping down from her lap and she caught it before it was late and was surprised at her quick reflexes for a split second.

'What did you just say?'

The old woman spoke, 'You are right Raju, she, with all her so called intelligence, is not even able to comprehend a simple question.'

She then turned to Ranjani and said in a matter of fact tone, 'Obviously, you are not alright and you are mentally disturbed. Do you feel like killing yourself because of your depression?'

What the heck! Such a direct and open subterfuge!

Ranjani rolled her eyes and glared at the duo and gave a hearty laugh. 'It's not depression. On the other hand,

I am euphoric. Yes! I do feel a killer's urge and I really want to kill someone, at least a couple of people, and I have absolutely no inclination to commit suicide. For the past two days I have been trying to decide on my first target.'

Inspite of her laughter, the anger in her huge eyes and the venom in her voice staggered the mother and son and they started slipping away in different directions- she, towards the kitchen and he, upstairs.

'Wait,' once again they were spellbound by her thunderous, commanding voice, which they probably were hearing for the very first time.

'I am leaving to my parents' place tomorrow. My father is not well and he needs me now.'

Raju came back alive first and reacted. In a stammering tone he said, 'No, we cannot permit you now. My sisters will be here to celebrate mother's eightieth birthday and you cannot go. I need you by my side during the function.'

Ranjani gave another laugh and asked in a taunting tone, 'Do I sound like seeking anybody's permission? It is just for your kind information; I *am* leaving at the earliest. The cook, your regular, will give you company during that stupid function too, or if that one would not do, you can bring in that other woman, your current girl friend, your ex-colleague's widow or that stupid, ugly, middle aged spinster, who calls herself a professional. You do have a handful of such worthless females to pick from! Just spare me!'

Raju took a step forward, gave her an indecisive look and turned towards his mother.

Again Ranjani went off, 'Don't worry about her and obviously she is aware of everything right from the start. She wouldn't mind anything as long as you keep pumping your money into her coffers. Am I right *ma?*' She now turned to her mother-in-law and accosted her, probably for the very first time ever.

With all contempt surfacing and over-powering, she moved a bit closer to her husband and hissed, 'Your mother is a bloody shit-eater. May you spend the rest of your life with her! You both deserve each other and nothing better.'

Raju took the next step towards her, his palm raised as if he was going to strike her. She bent down and slowly removed the bathroom slippers she was wearing, first from her right foot and then from the left, with firm deliberation.

The old woman gaped at the scene in total disbelief and with panic writ all over her face.

Ranjani threw her slippers outside the door, towards the gate. 'There is no point in wearing the slippers that keep pinching you, right?'

The violent jerk of the throw got her thumb caught in her thick gold chain with the *Thirumangalyam* dangling in front and it broke. The chain slid to her feet and the four golden beads and the two solid M- shaped blocks with *Siva Lingas* engraved on them, scattered all around.

One of the slippers landed right in front of the cook Swarna, who had just entered the premises and was closing the gate behind her. As she took an indecisive step forward, one of the beads bounced off the floor and came rolling towards her, which she picked up without thinking but stood rooted to where she was, on realizing what it was.

Ranjani deliberately collected the broken chain and the other pieces from the floor, walked in measured strides to the menial and just snatched the glittering piece out of her hand.

'That is my father's hard earned money. But I'll let you have those useless things as I don't need them anymore,' she pointed to the slippers lying askew, two meters apart. Her voice was taunting and sarcastic.

Slowly she turned to Raju, 'Anyway, she had started filling into my shoes long back and it suits all of us.'

She gave him a cold smile and he froze.

She walked past him into her room and started packing her things in the suitcases and cartons she had brought down from the junk room upstairs, the previous night, and had stacked under the cot. By then the old woman had slumped into a chair and started wailing and Raju rushed to her side and could be heard consoling her in a hushed voice.

Ranjani called up her son, who materialized within an hour with a pick-up van. He loaded the van with the help of the driver, who was also known to Ranjani as one of the beneficiaries of her son's benevolence. As the van drove away, she walked out of the house unceremoniously and without bothering to say goodbye to anyone, got on the pillion of the *Bullet,* which was already roaring.

'Let's move on!'

3

Emancipated

Shree gasped for breath and opened her eyes wide. She had broken into a cold sweat and in the diffused light she could see her milky white arms glistening. She was fully awake and still remembered every part of her weird dream. It was strange! Rather unusual! She never could recall any of her dreams though she dreamt a lot.

What was that? She could not understand anything.

The dream had her running with gay abandon. It was more like floating, as she could not feel her body. She knew that she was stark naked but felt as if she was fully covered. She looked down at herself saw colourful, misty blotches all over her body.

There were blues, browns, grays and fiery reds and somewhere she even found a couple of colourless patches. They seemed to emanate from her body but still formed part of her.

She thought she would not be totally free until she got rid of them. She rubbed herself and tried to peel them off but to her horror, chunks dropped off her body and vaporised, leaving gaping holes. She was them- those blotches!

She started screaming, wondering what she was made of and who she was. The blue was pale and nebulous. The bright red colour started blazing fierily and called out, 'You are me!'.

The pale blue then suddenly, grew intense, and like a protective blanket tamed down the fierceness of the red

Shree then had done a strange thing in the dream. She hugged herself and ended up with a handful of blotchy blobs. She shrieked loudly, 'I am in my elements! You are me!' The red blob burned fiercely then and she was enveloped in a frosty cold.

Then started the exhilarating performance of Shree, swirling with the colourful medley, enfolding her, enveloping her and enthralling her and she turned the performer of an invigorating dance. It encompassed the elements, the universe, the cosmos but not quite. The dance was within her and every movement was choreographed in her head, felt inside her, and presented by her exterior. She twirled and whirled, swished and whished, waxed and waned, assembled and disintegrated and finally enlarged and vanished as tiny specs.

That was when she had opened her eyes and sat upright on the bed.

She looked down and heaved a sigh of relief to find her body intact, wrapped around by her soft blue quilt. She calmed herself down and looked around. The digital clock on the table nearby showed 5:45:36.

Shree decided to start her day and went inside the bathroom. The image from her dream followed her everywhere and she was still in a dazed stupor.

She came out into the balcony with her huge mug of green tea. The quail in the bush adjacent to the compound wall was striking up a solitary chord. She once again went back into her dream, every bit of it and slowly something dawned on her. She recalled a conversation she had had with her brother Pradheep about a couple of years back.

Her father was terminally ill and the last few months had actually reversed roles for father and daughter. He had became a mere child depending on her for comfort and reassurance and she had remained by his side till the fateful day. She took great care not to let him know the personal strife that was tearing her apart. Relationship had soured and she had been seriously contemplating a legal separation from her spouse. All along, she could never admit that her father, who had been the source of her strength, inspiration and her entire being, had been cheated into making a wrong choice as far as her life partner was concerned. Now, at this juncture, she would never break his heart with the knowledge of this huge failure on both their parts and hasten him to his end.

Her brother had noticed everything long back and was shrewd enough to understand what she had been going through all these years. Yet he could not talk to her or do much to rescue her as long as she remained quiet in her futile effort to cover things up.

Yet, her father could not be fooled that easily and in spite of his pain and disorientation caused by the potent drugs that he was administered, he had read the signs of her miseries and just a few hours before he departed, he very casually called her.

'*Kannamma,* never ever go back to that house again. This is the place where you really *live*. Take care of yourself and *Amma*. You can always be *you* here.'

Shree was stunned and simply looked at him, tears brimming over and running down her cheeks. He continued in his soft voice, now strained by the pain,

'Remember, life is to live and not to battle. Sometimes it may start a little late but turns out to be rich. You are fifty-one. Now your time starts. Live it up. Live it to the full. Remember your favourite poem, *Ulysses?*'

She started chanting their favourite lines

> *I am a part of all that I have met;*
> *Yet all experience is an arch wherethro'*
> *Shines that untravell'd world whose margin fades*
> *Forever and forever when I move.*

'It's *gleams*, not *shines*.' He corrected her and she marvelled at the sharpness of his mind even when his senses were dulled by his excruciating pain. Well, that was the last of such conversations they both normally would have and he was gone in short of twelve hours.

The entire family had been bracing itself for this inevitable moment and even her mother retained her stoicism. Everyone else was surprised at the poise and dignity the family maintained during the funeral, which was devoid of any ritual as per father's wish; the profundity of the grief was weighing heavily on the mind of each of them, though.

Pradheep stood in the waist deep waters of the gushing *Bhavani*, with the urn containing father's ashes and called out to his sisters and mother who were standing on the bank, 'Want to touch *Appa* one last time?'

As if waiting for this invitation the three ladies rushed towards him, the older one supported by her daughters on either side. All the three touched the urn he was holding up to them, all at once, and immediately Shree felt a tremor running through her body. The entire scene presented a rather strange picture, four people and an *asthi kalsa!* She could feel the heaviness that had been weighing her down all her life, lifting up and taking flight into the distant skies.

She looked up and caught the glazed look in her brother's eyes and realized what he was going through.

The scene froze like a painted picture.

She gently said, 'Good bye *pa*. You are *there*. I am so happy for you.'

Shree snapped out of the scene first, suddenly withdrew her hand and started walking back to where Abi was standing on the bank, positioning himself in an unobtrusive fashion, yet watching the tableaux with great concern and interest. He just extended his hand and helped her up, not that she needed it, and looked at her. It was a look of understanding and acknowledging the sense of liberation she had just moments ago, experienced. He simply put a protective hand round her shoulder and walked her to the car parked at a distance. Her mother followed close behind, supported by her sister and her brother was trailing behind totally lost in thoughts, lost to the world.

Later, when she was sitting under the sky in the open terrace of their house late at night, Pradheep and Abi quietly joined her, each harbouring a glass of scotch in his hand.

Pradheep asked unceremoniously, 'What was that, *akka?*'

'I think, I now understand everything, the entire picture. You see *appa* was everything, and as far as I could see, he was the omniscience, the omnipotent and omnipresent, for even now I can feel his presence everywhere, like the *Sky*. *Amma* had out and out been patiently putting up with everything and everyone of us, and was well grounded, a personification of the *Earth*.

'I could survive the worst because I could maintain a characteristic stance. People needed my warmth and I cherished them but when they got too close or played with me, I burnt them like *Fire*. I am really a firebrand, fiery and furious. With our sister Jaishree, it has been different through and through. She is cool, meticulous and well-planned about everything in life. Like a river, decides on her course and meanders it. She is balmy and comforting like *Water*.

'On the other hand, you are the wandering spirit in the family with an insatiable thirst for travel inside and outside of you. You cannot be contained, and you explore all realms and fill up everything you take up with your presence like the invisible *Wind*.

'We are the elements and we complement each other and fill up each other. We are made of each other, don't you see? So must be everything and everyone else in the world.'

Shree stopped and looked at her brother with a fear she might not be making sense to him, but was relieved to see his bright smile of understanding, and he quipped 'You are talking *Advaita!*'

'Or even *Asimov* for that matter' interjected Abi.

'And that makes sense. I could feel the connect, but could not get it straight then,' continued Pradheep.

Was the dream a reminder of her future course of action or her innate yearnings to finally get reduced to her elemental self? She felt more of herself now in the absence of her father's subduing influence.

She heard her mother in the kitchen and minutes later the aroma of filter coffee heralded her entry into the balcony. She was due to leave for the US the next day and had come to Shree's small apartment, which was closer to the airport, with all her baggage, the day before.

Shree had moved into this new place, as she wanted to be rid of unwanted memories and unwanted people who kept running into her once in a way in her old locality. She had secured her freedom at last after a lot of fight and got the copy of the court order just the previous week. She had given up her job and was doing projects as a consultant, apart from giving guest lectures.

It was indeed a very special day, being the date of birth of her mother as well as her daughter-in-law, a strange coincidence indeed! Shree had planned a quite family get-together, not forgetting to include Thaman in the list of her close circle- just those people who mattered to her.

Abi came with his wife and child by around nine and Thaman followed closely. Thaman had been away on one of those long road-trips for more than two weeks and in spite of a little weariness, he was his usual boisterous self, laughing aloud, teasing Mili and entertaining the baby with his own rendition of *Old McDonald had a farm* with the sounds of all the animals. When he tried to trumpet like an elephant in the farm, even her mother burst out laughing. Initially the old lady had not liked him much and when she was alone with Shree she simply said, 'Don't you have even one friend who is normal?'

Shree had shot back, 'Normal people ditch their friend in need, for fear that they would be approached for help, especially normal women. They don't want to take chances, nor would they do anything that would jeopardize their reputation by associating with a woman who walked out of her marriage. I don't blame them. In most cases it is the husband who is scared that his wife would follow suit and hence keeps her away from me by casting aspersions.'

But eventually her mother had grown out of her initial prejudice and became very fond of Thaman.

As the day wore off, the house was filled with activities. Mili had transformed the entire place glowing with her own touch of artistry and aesthetics. She just rearranged the furniture, changed curtains and wall hangings, put insignificant things in odd places, including the baby's Bunny Rabbit and Talking Turtle. Strangely, the baby had developed a distinct dislike for dolls and dumb toys and would throw them away and wail for something more interesting, like an i-pad or a smart phone.

After quite a long time, Shree selected a *sari* for the evening and when she came out of her room in a white chiffon *sari* with deep blue patterns and with a matching pair of pearl studs, her mother's face brightened. She had brushed her short hair back and fastened a clip at the nape, yet loose strands were flying on either side of her face, accentuating her high forehead and dark eyes. Mili hugged her and said, 'I like you better this way *ma*.'

All of a sudden Mili ran inside, opened her handbag and came back holding something between her thumb and index finger. She stuck a small red *bindhi* dot on Shree's forehead between her dark brows, moved back a bit and utterly satisfied with the effect it had created, gave a big smile.

She turned towards Shree's mother and said, '*Paatti, amma* now looks pretty *na*?' The older woman's eyes welled up with tears and she heaved a big sigh. Experience has taught her that any remark of remorse or regret would draw sharp reaction from either her daughter or her grandson or both. Thaman was curiously watching this drama in silence, incongruous to his nature. When he saw Shree dressed very soberly and with care he could not take his eyes off her and stood spell-bound. He wanted to say something but felt choked. His mind took him back long afar and he felt lost and perplexed. Then, all on a sudden he got up and started searching for something or it looked, for someone rather. He looked behind the doors, the curtains, the fridge and under the cots and sofa and everyone of them was puzzled. He walked all over flailing his hands.

Shree was the first to come out of the confusion and laughed.

'Hey Thams, what's up?' Abi could not get it still.

'Dude, suddenly a friend of mine has gone missing, a real toughie, she is. May be, that elegant lady over there might know something. Let me check with her.'

As everyone started laughing, Shree approached him and gave a sharp slap on his shoulder, which made them all go nonstop once again.

The evening turned out to be a very pleasant one and they were all relaxed. There was a mood of celebration, but of nothing in particular, not even the birthdays. Only Shree realised that the reason for the jubilation was her new found freedom and the day she secured it, not long back, was still green in her memory.

When she emerged out of the *Power Room*, she heard the cooing and gurgling of the baby and Mili's incoherent babble along with.

'Mili, talk to her in real words. That's how she picks up the language. Give her something to imitate,' she gave a gentle reminder to the wonderful girl.

'Look *ma*, she has learned to blow bubbles and wouldn't stop doing it. She wants me to do the same along with her. She is becoming very insistent now-a-days. Very assertive, like her father, or more so like the grandma!'

Affectionately Shree draped her hands round her shoulders and took a peek at the rolly-polly baby in the crib. She had an air of independence, quite unlike any other baby her age, whom she had seen, including her own. She resisted the strong desire to lift her and cuddle her.

'Oh my God, you are ready! Just keep an eye on her and I'll change … or rather I'd do that after getting the little one ready'.

'Mili, should you come to that place? I don't want that bastard to cast a glance on either you or the baby. You know he is evil personified and can scare and scar one with just those festering eyes.'

Mili was crest fallen, 'Please *ma*, we all need to be there together. Only then, he would know the value of what he has lost and realise that there is nothing worth living for any further. It is your victory *ma*.'

Before Shree could respond, there was a huge clamour in the kitchen, obviously the noise of stacking the dirty dishes in the sink and Abi called out, 'Ladies, your breakfast is ready. Hurry, before it gets cold or eaten up!' It was rather a superfluous announcement as the appetizing aroma of toasts and cheese omelets wafted out of the kitchen and they could hear him setting the table.

Shree adjusted the merry-go round toy hanging above the crib. The baby could barely touch it but her efforts to grab it was always undaunted but at the same time unrewarded too. Anyway, she could be kept engaged for at least fifteen minutes and they both could get quiet a huge amount of task done in those precious minutes.

As expected, Abi had already started breakfasting. 'Have to get ready. Don't worry, I'll get the baby ready too. Both of you take your own sweet time', he said in a muffled tone with his mouth almost full and over that, he gave a broad grin.

Suddenly there was a hushed silence, which hung heavily among the three people, with each of them zoning out into a different territories.

Shree was fighting to stay calm and struggling to drown the familiar feeling of raw anger that was trying to break free and resurface, after quite a long passage of time.

Abi suddenly looked up, straight into her eyes, reached across and patted her hand, and said, 'It's all over.

Goodness gracious!' Rapidly his glance darted and rested on Mili, who was lost in her own thoughts, but then she just looked up, caught his eyes and smiled. He beamed affectionately at her. 'My dear girl, get ready fast. Don't delay all of us with your dreamy movements', he bantered.

Shree sent them both away to get ready and cleared the table. She needed to catch her breath a bit. She plugged in her earphones and just selected some piece of music at random without looking, more because she was not wearing her trendy glasses. Igor Stravinsky's *Rite of Spring* gave her a shudder and she was struck by the aptness of the theme- the sacrifice of the Fertility King. Really, it was going to be a good-riddance, the slaughter of the sterile demon today. Her fingers once again shuffled through the playlist and she settled with Dr. Balamuralikrishna's mellifluous rendition of *Nagumomu* in *Aaberi*.

Shree sat very straight on the grandfather chair and dissolved into the music, yet her inner mind stayed awake and alert for the events portended for the day.

Her final wait had just begun!

At the court, as usual, she had to wait long before her case was called, and after that, everything moved and ended fast. She thanked Advocate Mithra with all her heart and after signing one or two documents to get the copy of the decree, she finally shook hands with him and he wished her good luck, promised to stay in touch and left.

Mother and son came out and walked to the parking lot in total silence. They had strictly forbidden Mili to enter the building and pulling a long face she had agreed to spend time in the cafeteria or in the car entertaining the baby and waiting for their return. She had simply refused to listen to them both when they had tried to discourage her coming along.

Luckily, Shree's mother had arrived at the court at the last moment, in a taxi, without notice and declared, 'I had already decided to come, but knew you would not let me. So, I kept it a secret. After all, I must be of moral support to my daughter at such times.'

Abi, in his own way, sweet-talked her into keeping company to Mili and the baby and she was more than happy to spend around two hours with the little one, forgetting totally her original mission.

Mili saw them both approaching the car and got down with the baby. The great-grandmother had just dozed off. The three of them stood there for a moment in total silence. Looking visibly relieved, Abi stepped between the two of them and put his arms around both of them protectively, with the little one in the middle.

Surprised by the sudden move Shree just melted into the comforting fold.

Suddenly, she sensed Abi stiffening, followed his gaze and caught a glimpse of the man who had caused her to step into the court. He was crestfallen, yet trying to peek a look at the baby in Mili's hands. Mili too had by then seen him and instinctively covered the baby with the thin flannel, and all the three closed in cocooning the baby, totally invisible to all prying eyes. Shree had not taken her eyes off Rajmohan, who, now or at anytime, had meant nothing to her, and was totally surprised by his strange deportment. The smile on her lips froze and she looked at him straight with unsmiling eyes. She could sense him collapse internally and he was on the verge of breaking down, going down with tears on the shoulders of the young girl with him, probably one of his aides.

Shree's victory had been a perfectly complete one!

'Take care, both of you! Don't get too adventurous!' Abi loaded the *Highlander* with the last piece of baggage and closed the boot with a bang and called out to them. Shree kissed the baby fondly and handed her over to Mili.

'Take care, my dear. Eat well. Stay in touch!'

Thaman shook Abi's hand and patted his back. 'Don't you worry about your mom, Mr. Abinandh. She is my best friend, a special friend too. I guarantee hundred percent safety to her.'

Abi said, 'I am more worried about you. You are travelling with a tigress. Take care of yourself,' and burst out into his usual kind of hearty laughter.

Shree's mother had been gone overseas a little over a month. She left as planned, as soon as Shree's long-drawn legal battle had come to an end. When Thaman started making plans for his next trip, Shree had implored him to accommodate her in his plans. She needed a break, a change of scene and her travel-lust was getting the better of her, and finally he had to concede.

They both got into the vehicle and waved to the couple. Thaman started the engine. As they drove out of the city limits, he switched on the music system and Shree was pleasantly surprised to hear the soothing melody of *Ilayaraja -Nilaave vaa...*

She could feel all tension and anxiety easing out of her system and she closed her eyes, yielding herself completely to the music. After decades, she dropped all her reserve and defences and relaxed completely. Thaman was unusually quiet and she was very thankful for that. The deep slumber that she had been longing for enveloped her in its dark velvety folds. They moved on and the music just played.

> *'I travelled every country,*
> *I travelled in my mind.*
> *It seems we're on a journey,*
> *A trip through space and time.'*

FINALE

... comes back

Very slowly, she came out of the enveloping darkness. She did not have the heart to reach a state of complete wakefulness and leave the protective comfort that had enfolded her. Her head rested on something strong but gentle and some distant refrain had transported her to a soothing surrealistic realm. She opened her eyes and saw a familiar thing that had not belonged in her world for ages.

She could not understand where she was and when it was. She realised that she was in an upright posture, rather sitting on some soft seat enfolding her. Slowly she lifted her head and turned to her left in a bid to recapture the scene that had jolted her out on opening her eyes.

'Aha, I now see that Sleeping Beauty is up,' she heard the familiar voice coming from the right side in the hazy darkness.

She now took stock of the surroundings and asked, 'Where are we? Why have we stopped?'

'Well, you started nodding and finally slept on my shoulders. I didn't want to get distracted by your snoring. So, I got onto the service road, drove a little down and parked at this scenic spot.'

She looked around surprised, 'Scenic spot!'

Dr. Sashikala

'Well, it's height of summer. The lake that could have been here might have gone dry and probably that's why there is no other vegetation or creature around.'

She did not appear to hear him. Her eyes were glued to the specter of sight to her left.

She asked in a shaky voice, 'Where did that come from?' she pointed to it.

He coolly replied, 'It had been there for years. We have now come to it.'

'I have seen that. I know it.'

'Obviously. It is one of the many of its kind. All of them look more or less the same.'

Still, she looked distant and her senses were full of the tamarind tree in front.

'Well, let me tell you something that happened long back under one such tree. There was this inquisitive boy and everyone in that place told him not to go to a particular spot because it was the favourite haunt of a Mohini. So he wanted to catch a glimpse of her and worse still captivate her and went to the forbidden glade, well prepared, to make her his possession. He waited and waited but never could see her. He was relentless and the place became his haunt. One day, as he was about to give up as usual, she came gliding down and he was enchanted the moment he set his eyes on her, though she

212

was not in the least like anything he had anticipated. But, she was enchanting in her own way… with an ethereal quality. She did not fit into that eerie surrounding with that imposing tree in the background. Well, why was she there? What was she doing?' He stopped on catching the gleam in her eyes in the semi-darkness of the dusk.

'She was waiting to get a glimpse of the Muni*', she filled in, in a tone devoid of any emotion.*

'Aha… now it's clear.' He continued, 'Yes the Mohini *was waiting for the* Muni *but she never saw him.'*

She picked up the thread now. 'He was right there all along, she could never see him. But she felt him close by, yet did not find him.'

He cleared his throat, which was choked with emotions. 'But he saw her, captured her in his heart and later in a canvas.'

'Then what happened?' she asked with her eyes half-closed again.

'He decided to follow her and possess her. But couldn't do that and let go of her.'

'Why?'

'He was by then possessed by her. Yet he loved her so much that he decided to let go of her.'

'That was real bad… bad for her.' She added in a hushed voice. 'Was she gone? You lost track of her?'

'More or less, saw her once.'

'Why didn't you reclaim her?'

'She was in captivity. Possessed and harassed by a Rakshasa. Just gave her some solace by singing to her… benumbing her sensitivity so as to help her escape her reality, though only for fleeting moments.'

'Why didn't you come to my rescue?'

'You obviously did not expect to be rescued.'

She sat up straight. The reality slowly dawned on her.

'But how…? Thaman? No, it cannot be… Raghu?

'Yes Ji… Gina, it is Raghu, Raghothaman. How do you remember Raghu after all these years?'

'Last month, as I was helping amma to clear up her place, I found it.'

'The sweet blue bamboo guitar?' he could not hide his disbelief.

'Yes. It was all wrapped up in a quilt and was hidden from all eyes on the loft upstairs. And when I saw that, I couldn't help yearning to go back there.'

'You are there. Or else Raghu would not have materialised.'

She sighed, 'Yes, but he has come a little too late.'

'When I saw you then, that day, listening to my band, I realised what I had done to you. I hadn't liberated you but on the contrary pushed you deep into hell, tethered you- such a spirited person- to an eon of lifeless life. I could never forgive myself. Your vacant stare haunted me these past years.' Again his voice broke and she gently patted his forearm in an effort to reassure him, but stayed very quiet, her right palm resting on his left hand.

'Again, when I saw you at my exhibition and when I shook your hand, I knew that you were that same Shreeranjani again, my age-old friend, Gina, but much stronger and too different '

'But I don't understand, why...'

'Why I did not re-establish our previous connections. Be honest with me! Would you have remembered a long forgotten friend who had nothing to revoke your memory with?'

'So, you started all over again?'

'No, this time I helped you to get started, for I was already in full throttle.'

She laughed. It sounded light but whole-hearted. They sat quiet for a few minutes. She had gone deep inside herself and he was watching her face with rapt interest.

After what seemed like ages, he gently turned his palm upward and took her hand into it and she turned right, looking straight up into his eyes.

'Gina, it had been dull all along, going on trips all alone. You have made a difference this time and showed me what life could be when you share your ventures, the good ones as well as those disastrous, with someone you know so well. Can we do it often?'

'You bet! Never ever think of any trip without me. The road is bound to get more and more lonely. Let's take it together, at our pace, at all times, as partners in all adventures.'

'Yes, at our own pace, all the time', he murmured softly

All on a sudden his voice caught the exhilarating excitement that he was right then experiencing, 'Well, what is more adventurous than life, my dear?'

She simply smiled and squeezed his hand. After a couple of minutes of profound and comforting silence, he slowly disentangled his hand, returned her smile with a broad grin and started the engine. As it came to life, she gently leaned her head on his shoulder and closed her eyes.

The tamarind tree started receding behind them and became a spectre of their past.

****